NO TIME
LIKE TOMORROW

ALSO BY TED WHITE

Secret of the Marauder Satellite
Spawn of the Death Machine
The Great Gold Steal
Sideslip (with Dave Van Arnam)
The Jewels of Elsewhen
The Sorceress of Qar
Phoenix Prime
Android Avenger

NO TIME
LIKE TOMORROW

by Ted White

Crown Publishers, Inc.   New York

F

W58N

C.2.

Printed in the United States of America.
Library of Congress Catalog Card Number: 71–75074.
Published simultaneously in Canada by General Publish-
ing Company Limited.
Second Printing, June, 1970

This one is for
Lester del Rey
and for
Erik van Lhin,
Philip St. John,
Kenneth Wright,
and all the others . . .

NO TIME
LIKE TOMORROW

Chapter One

FOR FRANK MARSHALL IT WAS very much like dying. There was no time for thoughts, no time to react. One moment he was standing in his backyard, staring at the nighttime sky, watching for the sudden sparking of a meteorite or the fast-moving dot of a satellite—the next he was caught in a maelstrom that defied his senses.

Later he would try to explain it, but if he satisfied others, he never satisfied himself. "I don't know . . . I had the thought, maybe they've really dropped the Bomb, but I didn't even have time to really think *that*. It was so—quick. It, well, it just didn't seem to take any time at all. Just—*bang!*" and he'd clap his hands together. "Like that."

And on another occasion the Syncom labmen would wire him into a luxuriously comfortable chair and replay his memories all over again for him—this time in slow motion. He would scream, but afterward tell them, in a shaky voice, "It was dark, you know—nighttime. But the darkness when I was looking at the sky, that was alive: It was real. When *it* happened, it was like somebody threw a switch on me, somebody turned everything off. Or, maybe . . . maybe turned *me* off. No color, no depth, no light, and—no darkness. Nothing at all. I can't describe it, you know. I can't even remember it, really. It made me feel—" and he would shudder, relaxing only after one of the men had pressed an injector against his arm. A familiar spot of coldness on his skin, and then his emotions would seem to calm, and he would feel a greater distance from the experiences he had just relived inside himself.

"It made me feel like I was dead," he would repeat, quietly. "Or, like it must feel to be dead, I guess. No awareness, not even inside myself, but yet knowledge that something was happening to me. Do you see what I mean?

"My body seemed very light, as though every part of it was being pulled in every direction. And then, of course, I was . . . here."

Here.

Frank Marshall was born in Georgetown Hospital, Washington, D.C., July 9, 1951. He'd lived with his family for eighteen years in a quiet suburban city in Virginia. His family were "locals"—one of the relative few among the highly transient population that worked directly or indirectly for the federal government—and he had grown from a rather pudgy boy into a stocky adolescent in the same familiar, dull, comfortable surroundings he had known all his life.

Not quite six feet tall—one of the secret banes of his life— Frank weighed 185 pounds, and with his heavy physique could easily have tried out for the school football team. But he was too easy-natured, too slow-moving and uncoordinated, and when the coach or a friend would mention it, he'd shrug, smile a little, and drop the subject.

He kept his hair cut short, despite the modern fads for longer hair. His thick brown hair was totally unruly when he let it grow longer than an inch or two, and at times he would stare at himself in the bathroom mirror and wonder, despondently, why he couldn't have been taller, thinner, and with one of those lean faces that seemed to excite the girls. Good buddy Frank stared back at him from wide brown eyes and a face that betrayed not a care in the world, and seemed to tell him, "Forget it, fellow. Stay loose. Don't sweat it."

And that was "here" until August 2, 1969. And then, without warning, it wasn't.

There was a moment of infinite suspension, and then, as though it had never been, he found himself tottering for a firm footing on broken turf that was collapsing under him—in the middle of a vast and brightly lit room.

2

He could not help staring, even as he still struggled for his balance. Surrounding him were lights and faces, and beyond them burnished walls and crazy shadows. It was like something out of a bad horror flick. Under him, a mound of dirt, crowned with broken clods of turf and two familiar flagstones. One of the flagstones was whole, but the other had its corner cut off as cleanly as if it had been butter cut by a hot knife. He'd helped lay them both in their backyard when he was eight.

"Nyrda! Ya ful! Spa fon?"

He jerked his head up. The words were meaningless, but the tone was angry: hostile and accusing.

A man strode into the circle of lights. He was dressed in a jumpsuit of some sort of reflective, metallic material. It shimmered as he moved, like liquid. Thick black goggles were pushed up on his forehead, leaving red lines circling his eyes. His skin was swarthy, his hair black and thick, close-cropped. He wore muttonchop sideburns that followed his square jawline almost to his bare chin.

There was a background of jabbering now, but the man paid no attention to it. He dropped to his knees, and poked his finger at a clod of earth. An earthworm wriggled from it, and the man hastily jerked back his hand.

Frank staggered back a little, his feet sinking into the loose dirt and dislodging some of it. The man looked sharply up at him. *"Squa tront?"* he asked.

Frank shook his head. "I—I don't understand you," he said. He stared around him at the circle of men now drawing closer. All wore the same brightly metallic jumpsuits and goggles. The air seemed to thicken in Frank's nostrils, and his arms and legs grew very heavy. For a moment he felt as though he was drowning.

Then he fainted.

When he regained consciousness, he was lying in a bed. It was a very restful bed. It seemed to shape itself accommodatingly around him, holding him snugly and comfortingly. He opened his eyes to see a portion of a room in deep shadow, and thus lulled fell into a more normal slumber.

When he awoke again, he no longer felt tired, and the bed no longer seemed quite so seductive. Bright sunlight streamed in

3

from somewhere behind and over his shoulder, making the room a cheery explosion of yellows and oranges. For a moment he did not care where he was, and he felt his usual early-morning eager-to-be-up elation. Then he began looking around at the room.

Although rather featureless—there seemed to be no furniture in the room but the bed—at first glance, he seemed to be in a very normal room, not unlike his own.

But that was only at first glance.

There were no doors.

The angles were wrong.

The sunlight was too stark, too strong.

He sat up, a sudden motion that was almost absorbed by the curious bed that folded itself around his elbows.

Behind him, a low, wide window and a view of rich blue sky and blinding sun. Before him, walls that did not join each other at right angles. His eyes seemed to wrench as he tried to reconcile the perspectives. Then, suddenly, it all fell into place. The side walls were not parallel. The room was like a wedge with the point cut off. He was staring at the smaller of the two ends.

The sheet had fallen to his waist and he realized, belatedly, that he had no clothes on. It added to his growing discomfort.

As he stared at the blank wall facing him, a door suddenly appeared in it and began to open.

He let himself flop back into the bed. The bed *rippled* as he hastily pulled the sheet that covered him up to his neck.

A cart wheeled through the door, followed by a girl.

"Shir tag," the girl said with a brief smile, pushing the cart up to the bedside.

"I—" he said. He gave her a bewildered smile. "Listen, can you speak English? Can you tell me where I am? What's going on here?"

Her only reply, as she fiddled with the cart, was a puzzled frown. He tried to watch her, without appearing to do it in an obvious way.

He couldn't guess her age, but she didn't seem much older than he. Her hair was dark and close-cut, almost boyishly short. It reminded him of the fad his mother had gone through, when she had tried the "Italian look" and his father had hit the ceiling. Her skin was an olive that might be a deep tan or her natural color. Her

4

face was rounded, but slender, and without makeup. Her eyes hinted of exotic background, but her nose was short, almost pug-nosed, upturned, and cute. Her expression was very reserved, almost shy, and yet with a strange hint of mischief lurking behind it.

Her clothes reminded him of period-piece movies. Full of ruffles, high-necked and full-skirted, they concealed all of her figure but her narrow waist. They seemed to be made of many layers of dresses, the outermost of a transparent material, the underlayers shading into aqua. The effect was to surround her with a shimmering layer of translucency.

She'd made a shelf spring from the side of the cart, and extended it out over the bed. From the cart she took a flat box. As she set the box on the shelf, she touched its side and a lid sprang open. The aroma of rich food spilled out into the room, and Frank felt his stomach contract suddenly in a spasm of hunger.

The girl looked at him again, and back to the food. Then, surprisingly, she blushed. Her cheeks seemed to be glowing when she turned away and went to the door. The back of her neck was also red.

Her dress swished as she moved quickly to the door and peered cautiously around it. Then, touching it, she closed it, and the wall was once more blank and featureless.

The color had not left her face when she returned to him. Leaning over, she dipped two fingers into the open box of food, and then thrust them at his mouth.

Frank let his mouth drop open in surprise. Then he was tasting a thick, rich, gravy-like stuff. It tasted meaty, and yet unlike any sauce he had ever tasted before. His lips closed over her fingers, and they seemed slender and soft as she withdrew them. Her nails, his tongue discovered, were kept as short as his own.

He felt his own face growing hot. There was something embarrassingly, indecently intimate in this strange feeding. The girl seemed as aware of this as he was, and that only made it worse. But when she dipped her fingers into the box again, he opened his mouth willingly.

Her fingers were still in his mouth when the doors snapped open. The girl gave a startled gasp of surprise and jumped back from the bedside.

Beyond, in the doorway, stood a man and a woman.

The man looked neither young nor old. His face was the

same olive tan as the girl's, and unlined, but his shoulder-length hair was thickly salted with gray. He wore thigh-hugging pants and a tunic held with a wide sash at the waist. His pants were black, his tunic royal purple. He looked like he'd stepped almost directly out of a Douglas Fairbanks late-show movie. All he lacked was a sword at his side.

The woman, dressed in modest black, hung back as the man strode into the room.

"Nir svboda! Yu shir amatact, Dorian?"

The girl paled, as though slapped. She shook her head, dumbly, then dropped her eyes, her shoulders slumping.

The man spoke to her in slow, patient tones. She answered in brief monosyllables. He pointed to the door. The woman standing there moved quickly and deferentially to one side. The girl nodded. The man turned and walked back through the door. He did not look back. Defeated, the girl followed him. Then the door closed.

The older woman remained. Her skin was darker, and her face impassive. She stared for a moment at the closed door, as if by doing so she could follow the other two beyond it, shrugged, and turned to regard Frank.

Frank felt his head throbbing with questions, the answers to which he despaired ever knowing. The alien words still hung, echoing, in the air, and with them the sense of intrusion, of being in the wrong place at the wrong time that had been growing within him. Strong emotions had been expended here, and to what purpose he knew not.

The woman leaned over the bed, dipped her carefully manicured fingers into the still open box, and then extended them to Frank.

"It was a shocking sight," Damon told him later. "I was shocked to see Dorian herself feeding you." But that was after the man had returned with two techmen and the machine.

After the woman had fed him, she wheeled the cart from the room and left him alone. Immediately, Frank was restless. The strange gravy had not only satisfied his hunger, it had also stimulated him into the eager desire to be up and about.

But he was totally undressed under the single sheet that covered him, and there were no clothes in sight. So he waited, chaffing,

6

for what had to be more than an hour, expecting that at any moment the invisibly sealed door might snap open again—while the door remained steadfastly shut.

Finally he kicked free the sheet and climbed out of bed.

Feeling uncomfortable and uneasy, he pulled the cover sheet from the bed and wrapped it around him loosely, toga-fashion. Then he went to the window and stared out.

The window was wide, but not high. It seemed to be laminated of multiple layers of glass. The scene below helped to explain why.

Below were bare rock and dazzlingly white snow.

Bare shoulders of naked, primal rock thrust up from valleys of snow. The sun, high overhead, seemed somehow very close, for as far as his eyes could see the peaks of savage, desolate mountains fell away. He seemed to be high in a tower on the roof of the world.

Overhead and on the horizon were thin curlicues of diaphanous cloud-streamers, streaked against the glowing dark blue sky. Below, between the more distant jutting peaks arranged so vertiginously beneath him, thicker banks of lower clouds made rolling valley floors. They were almost as white as the nearby snow, but reflected rainbow glints where the sun struck their billows at odd angles.

It was impossible to see anything of the outside of the building he was in, but, Frank estimated, he was no less than ten floors above the mountain peak upon which the building apparently rested.

The snow was drifted bare of jutting ridges of black rock, and caught elsewhere in wind-rifts like frozen waves upon the sea. There were few shadows at this time of day, but yet he thought he could be sure of one last puzzling fact: There were no signs of human presence upon the snow—no tracks, no shoveled paths, nothing to indicate that man had ever set foot out there.

The room was warm, even the tiles of the floor warm against his feet, but yet he shivered.

Where was he?

What impossible thing had happened to him? The memory of that cavernous room, where lights and goggled men alike had stared at him, returned to him now. But it was more like a fragment of a nightmare than a real memory.

7

He tried to let his mind range back, back before that sharp break in reality which had brought him, and a portion of his backyard, here, to this place, wherever it was . . .

He had eaten supper, called Betti on the phone, talked with her for half an hour without saying anything, talked with her about absolutely inconsequential, meaningless things after she'd told him she couldn't go out with him Friday night, so that it wouldn't seem he was hanging up immediately. Then he'd watched TV a bit, gotten bored, and wandered out into the backyard to brave the mosquitoes and see if anything interesting was going on in the sky that night.

Frank had been an amateur astronomer, back in grade school and junior high, and later a member of the school astronomy club before it degenerated into a science club for lack of interest. Those were the days when men were first getting a toehold on space, and the two-man orbital flights, the space walks, everything was new and astronauts earned ticker-tape parades, and space was exciting. Those were the days when every launch—even the most routine—was televised live from the Cape, no matter what the hour.

He'd been late to school the day they'd broadcast the live Surveyor TV pictures of the moon, and when the personnel at Pasadena's Jet Propulsion Labs broke into cheers and congratulatory handshakes, he'd felt an awe that made the hair at the back of his neck bristle, and an excitement that almost moved him to tears. *How wonderful, how marvelous, to see live TV pictures broadcast from the moon!*

And you could still step into your backyard, and on a clear night you might sight any number of tiny specks of light moving rapidly across the starscape—Comsat satellites, weather-relay satellites, military spy satellites on polar orbit, abandoned booster rockets —hundreds of bits of man-made debris already littering orbits around Earth. And you could stand very still and watch, and sight the sudden stars, and try to imagine the size and shape and purpose of these artificial satellites, and feel a thrill in knowing that man, anchored since the beginning of his eternity to the face of this planet, had put them there.

It had been a warm night, muggy as summer nights in Virginia often were, and from across the back fence came the purr of the Kramers' air-conditioner, and from much closer the high-pitched whine of a mosquito dive-bombing his ear. His neck ached from holding his head tilted back, and he groped with his feet for the flagged patio area, where he could recline on the sun lounge.

He had still been staring upward when it had happened.

What had *happened?*

He still faced the window and the desolate scene below when the door snicked open again. He turned, his foot catching the sheet where it trailed on the floor, and he stared into the gray eyes of the tall man who had taken away the girl.

Behind him were two men, pushing a cart. They followed him into the room, then paused.

The gray-haired man had changed his clothes. Now he wore knickers-like trousers, tucked into high suede boots. A blood-red jacket did not entirely close over a white shirt with thick ruffles down its front. Again he reminded Frank of a character from a melo-dramatic movie.

In contrast, the men pushing the cart were dressed in brightly reflective jumpsuits. The sight of them was jarring. They brought a dark hint of nightmare with them into the sunny room.

They also brought a machine, upon the cart.

The gray-haired man gestured at Frank. His expression was stern, but not unkind. It was obvious that he wanted Frank back on the bed.

Frank looked back and forth between the man and the other two—and their machine. The machine drew and held his fascinated gaze. It was a simple cube of porcelain white, with rows of switches and various wires and tubes connected to its oddly spaced knobby projections, and it was, in its very hospital-like innocence, the most frightening object Frank had ever seen.

Just what was it they intended to do to him with that thing? His hackles rose, and he felt a low growl in his throat. *No.* He shook his head and backed slowly away.

Gray-hair barked an impatient noise, and made another ges-ture at the bed.

It was a small room. Frank shook his head again as he felt the cool glass of the window at his back. He wondered what might happen if he tried to break it.

They gave him no chance. The two men in jumpsuits moved quickly, like a well-rehearsed team, one to each side of him. A small metal cylinder gleamed for a moment in the hand of the one on his right. The man pressed its end against Frank's bare arm, and before Frank could shake free, he felt a brief numbing cold at that spot.

They were holding him, and he couldn't move. He tried to jerk his head around to stare at what they'd done to his arm, but his head would not move either. Black spots seemed to swim up at him from the floor, confusing him. It was all very dreamlike, very strange . . .

They put him on the bed and arranged the sheet over him again. He could see only the ceiling. The sun no longer came directly in the window. There were shadows on the ceiling. He heard a sound and knew the cart was being wheeled to his side, and a great hand seemed to clamp upon his chest for a moment as he fought his panic.

With surprisingly gentle hands, the two men began fitting wires to his arms, chest, and legs. Then a skeletal helmet was fitted over his head, and he felt a tingling at his temples. But he could no longer sort out the real sensations from the unreal, and he was still uncertain about the tingling when a sudden intense light flashed before his eyes, wiping out all sight of the ceiling overhead. He tried to blink his eyes shut, but the flash came again. Blackness followed.

He returned to consciousness to find the helmet and wires, the two men in jumpsuits, and the machine all gone. The man with gray hair stood at the foot of his bed. His mouth opened and he spoke, in the same harsh, guttural syllables as before. Frank heard him, and felt an overwhelming dizziness engulf him. His thoughts seemed to splinter and then regroup, and unanswered questions, the source of which he did not know, echoed in his brain.

"Do you understand me now, Frank Marshall?" the man had asked.

And Frank had.

Chapter Two

FOR DORIAN THE DAY HAD begun with a dream.

It was not a dream of the detailed sort that one remembers upon awakening, but the mood of the dream seemed to linger on, in the recesses of her mind, overwhelming her at odd moments with troubled thoughts and vague emotions. When she awoke, she could recall nothing of what she had just been dreaming, but she felt a sense of loss, a loss so keen that it made her want to cry.

It wasn't the first. She'd been having these dreams for several years now: heartaching dreams, dreams that made her feel an anticipation for something not real, not seen or understood.

"All young ladies such as yourself, My Miss Dorian," her governess had told her, "they all have dreams . . ." And the old woman had chuckled fondly at the thought.

"But that's silly, Gam'ma," Dorian had scolded her heatedly, using her childhood name for the woman. "I've had dreams all my life, but just—dreams. Like the stories you used to read to me. Sometimes they were scary, and sometimes they were funny, but just dreams. Now . . ."

"Now you're a young lady," her governess had said. "And now the dreams change. . . . Ah, I remember the yearnings I felt when I was little more'n your own age. . . ."

"Yearnings, Gam'ma?"

The old woman had clucked her tongue to herself and bowed

11

her head. "Such things are not proper to speak of to one of your station, My Miss Dorian," she'd said, and she would say nothing more.

But the dreams had persisted. Vague, languorous, too mistily thin to hold their shape in her memories after waking, they left only the afterimages, the strange feeling of tearful sadness at their passing. It was going to be one of those days. There were a few almost every month, when she would mope listlessly through her waking hours, to the exasperation of everyone around her. They would wring their hands and look at the ceiling and mutter about "Highborn young girls and their moods!" and she would ignore them.

She kicked back the covers from her large pneumoflex bed, and touched the button in the headboard that would summon Alceé, her personal maid.

Alceé took her cue from Dorian's distant stare and moody silence, and assisted her young charge to dress with a minimum of chatter. Alceé was middle-aged, thick-waisted, and dressed in simple servant black. And she looked upon Dorian as Dorian herself did upon her pet kitten.

After Alceé had fed her, Dorian prepared herself to greet her parents. It was a largely ceremonial gesture, and one that had become a meaningless ritual to her, but it was too firmly ingrained within her habits to be ignored, even if she should actually consider of it. And a proper young lady, heiress of the largest controlling corporation in the System, would never think of being rude to her elders, most certainly not to My Sir Damon and My Lady Grellian of Syncom.

Properly gowned, Dorian left her apartments and took a drop shaft down to the Grand Level. When she stepped out, Alceé and one of the apprentice servants in tow behind her, she found her parents already holding audience.

Duke Alexander, her father's younger brother, gave her a sharp frown from across the vast room. She was late again. She looked away from him. He was a drone, one of the Heirs who would never inherit, could never govern, but who was always to be found at functions dressed and acting as though all authority was his. She dismissed him from her mind, and went with as little haste as she properly could to her parents.

My Sir Damon was seated behind a desk which appeared to be, and was, a solid rectangular block of marble. Standing before him was a man dressed in the somber hues and simple cut of managerial clothing. The man seemed ill at ease and perhaps even perspiring a little in the cool, dry, regulated atmosphere of the great hall. That, or his skin was naturally oilier than most.

My Lady Grellian stood behind her husband and to one side. It was her habit to witness all audiences. She rarely ever spoke during one, but Dorian was well aware that in the private apartments of her parents her mother was capable of expressing herself forcefully and to good effect. It might appear that she was there for ceremony only, but her mind was quite as sharp as Damon's, and they made an excellent team. It was Dorian's private hope she might some day fulfill a similar function of her own, although when she'd confessed this once to Albert, her tutor, the man had laughed indulgently and chided her about her low marks in Admin Science.

"Ah, Dorian," said her mother, smiling slightly.

"My Sir, My Lady," Dorian said, curtsying. Her servants rustled in unison with her.

"Dorian," her father said, nodding. He gestured across his desk at the manager. "Manager Herron, my daughter, Dorian."

"Sir," she said, only nodding this time.

"My Miss Dorian," the man replied, bowing low.

Her mother smiled again, her father gave her another, final nod, and she turned to recross the great room.

"Every time you're late, you disrupt things," Alexander hissed at her in passing.

She stuck out her tongue at him and swept regally into the waiting drop-shaft cubical. The two women in black had barely managed to follow her before the doors snapped shut. As the smooth pressure of upward acceleration pressed the floor against her feet, her expression was already once more distant, her eyes again focused upon a moment she had dreamed only and could not recall.

"What am I to *do* with you, child?"

"Oh, Albert," she said, wearily.

"You have these days when you are simply impossible," replied her tutor. He was a small, rotund little man with pure white hair so thin and fluffy that it seemed to float in a halo over his pink bald spot. He had not changed in all the years she could remember him. His red face was perpetually good-humored, even when, as now, he was scolding her. He'd ignored her title. When he was impatient with her obstinance, he would treat her as simply a rather willful, balky little girl.

His rich lavender suit was spotted with food. His suits were always spotted with food, even though he rarely wore the same suit for more than half a day. Just now her eye was fixed on a small spot of something rust-brown just under his collar.

"*Think,* now: Neillson's Corollary. What *is* it?" he asked again.

She tore her gaze from the spot and raised it. His large eyes stared guilelessly back at her. "I don't remember," she said. "I just don't remember. I don't *want* to remember. I'm bored." She yawned. "Numbers bore me. Math bores me. Managerial cost-effectiveness bores me. And you're starting to bore me." She stood up.

He winced, a fleeting expression, but she caught it. "Oh, Albert," she said, flinging herself at his knees, rocking him back in his chair. "I'm sorry. I really am. I didn't mean to say that. I was very wicked, truly I was."

He nodded. "You are indeed, at times. Come now, stand up. It's not proper. What if Alceé should come in here and see you like that with your head in my lap? You'd horrify twenty years from her age. Now, now—no tears."

She rose and walked to the window, pulling back the heavy drapes. Bright sunlight spilled into the room, and that was wrong. She'd expected a gray overcast. It was a gray sort of day for her, and the sunlight was all wrong. It washed up against her gray moods and lapped away at them. But she couldn't close the drapes again. That's what the sunlight did to her—it was insidious.

The snow sparkled and glinted, little streamers of the dry powder wafting across the rocks as the wind drifted it. The sky was an electric blue. Too bright, too vivid, too ordinary and familiar. It made her feel like a little child again, and she didn't want to feel that way. Her lingering moods were slipping away from her, dissipating in the bright light.

"I don't mind saying that makes it a bit cheerier in here," Albert said.

"I don't want to study anymore," she said, turning away from the window.

The sunlight carved bright patterns on the thickly carpeted floor, and climbed the old man's purple legs almost to his knees. His

14

upper body and face were lost in the gloom of the shadows; the light of the room's lamp was lost in the glare of sunlight.

"Ah, what then?" he asked.

"Tell me the gossip."

"Alceé tells you everything," he said, his voice smiling.

"No, she only tells me about the servants and all their petty intrigues. She just tattles. Tell me about the corporation. Who was that man—Herron?—who was here this morning?"

"Herron? Hmmm . . . A most saddened man. He was in charge of the star-drive program."

"Tell me about it?"

The old man smiled, indulgently. "Tell you another story, Dorie? Something to amuse you when you're bored? But these things are real, you know. And they're tied up in dry, fusty old topics like math and science and corporate management. Dull things; you wouldn't want to hear about them."

"Oh, please, Albert. You know that's not so. Please . . . ? Tell me about the star-drive program and about Herron and why he should be so sad. Tell me what happened?"

"There, there, my dear. Begging hardly becomes you, My Miss Dorian. It does not suit your position."

"All right," she said, suddenly laughing. "If that's the game, then, as an Heir and Your Miss Dorian, I *command* you tell me!"

"That's better," the old man said, nodding sagely, eyes atwinkle. "Never forget your station. I may be your tutor, but you cannot behave beyond this room as you do in it. Best learn your proper habits."

She sighed. "And end up with a lecture! You can be the most evasive man in the world, Albert!"

He laughed. "True. But I'll tell you the story, anyway. What do you know of the star-drive program?"

"Nothing. I thought star-drive was impossible."

"And so it is . . . and so it is. The lack of any real star-drive has kept us trapped within our solar system for some five centuries of space travel, now. And I have no doubt that the first man to invent a true faster-than-light drive to other systems will be the most important man in *any* system. The value of a working star-drive is incalculable. Ahh . . . escape from our own solar system at long last! Escape from these dreary overcrowded worlds! How wonderful it would be to walk upon the face of a world where the wind blew fresh in one's face, where as far as one could see, horizon to horizon, the land was open and free and untrampled by another man's foot! Yes, indeed . . ."

"You *said* star-drive is impossible," Dorian reminded him.

"And it is—for the present, at any rate," he sighed. "Oh, we've sent a few ships out in the last three centuries. One-way missions—suicide missions, in my opinion. We tried cold-sleep suspended animation; we tried one ship large enough to contain a self-sustaining ecology and several generations of crew; we've tried unmanned drone-ships with sending equipment—oh, we've tried almost every way of breaking out of our shell, but the simple limitations of distance are too great. It takes too long. Even the nearest star is centuries away, by conventional means of space travel. Unless man can invent a means of traveling faster than light, he will simply never expand to other star-systems.

"However," the old man said, clearing his throat and continuing, "you may be sure that every major corporation in this system is actively seeking the drive. Every one of them has a star-drive project, just as we do. And each and every one is staffed by teams who hope to be the first!

"Theoretically, at least, the star-drive is not impossible. For centuries, scientists have theorized f-t-l particles. These particles, according to theory, would arrive at their destination *before* departure from their point of origin. There's quite a body of math built up around the notion, but I'm afraid it's well beyond you, Dorian."

"It sounds like nonsense to me," Dorian replied with a toss of her head. "Something that arrives before it leaves? That's just a verbal paradox." She knew that much, anyway.

"Perhaps. But it produces results," Albert said. "Some sort of results, anyway."

A man five hundred years old! The thought dizzied her. "It was a blow for Herron, but he may salvage something from it," Albert had said. "They've succeeded in dating the time-traveler. He dates from between 1900 and 2000, Oldstyle. That makes him from around five centuries ago—the dawn of technological enlightenment."

Now she pushed the food cart along the hall and tried to imagine to herself what he must look like. Short and stubby and hairy, a big black mane and black beard, curly fur on the backs of his hands . . . A shiver went down her back, and she wondered what she was doing here in this high bare corridor.

She'd found Wilma wheeling the food, and she had suddenly and impulsively decided to take it in herself, leaving the puzzled woman standing behind. It was lowborn of her to assume a servant's task, but it had seemed like something exciting and amusing to do at that moment; now she wondered. Those days were before space-age civilization! He might be little more than a beast; he might leap at her and attack her. Dorian had a vivid imagination and it made up for a cloistered existence. It took all her remaining will to thumb the door to the man's room open and enter.

She paused, and stared.

Why, he was so young! He was no older than Elton. His hair was short, like a tech's, but he had a strange look—his eyes bothered her. They seemed to stare so directly that they made her feel uncomfortable. She wasn't used to people who didn't lower their eyes in her presence. And the way he clutched the sheet over him—as though he might be afraid of *her.* She wanted to laugh, and that broke the tension within her. Instead she gave him a brief smile and said, "Good day." She wasn't scared anymore.

He spoke to her. The sounds made syllables, and the syllables were connected as words. The words appeared to be set in sentences, and were not at all the animal grunts she still half-expected, but it was all a jumble of nonsense: noise. She frowned at him, and wheeled the cart up to his bedside.

Now what? Should she wait for Wilma? Would Wilma come? Well, she could set out the food; she'd done that much with her own hands before. She made the shelf spring out, and set the container on it. His eyes followed every movement she made. It frightened her a little, to be so close to a totally strange man, alone, he in a bed like this, but it made the skin at the base of her neck tingle in a not entirely disagreeable fashion. *Could she . . . ?*

She felt the heat come to her face as she glanced back at the open door. Wilma hadn't come. Could she, might she—*feed him?*

She felt herself blushing furiously, her skin crawling and prickling with the heavy rush of blood. It was unheard of! No Heir had ever lifted a tool to help himself, much less given assistance to a person of lower station in all her life!

On the other hand . . . what *was* this time-traveler's station? He was unique to this time and this world. And . . . mightn't that elevate him to a station in life at least approximating her own . . . ?

She thumbed the door shut after hastily checking the corridor. It had been empty. Wilma had disappeared. It was just as well.

She returned to the bed, her stomach a tight knot of excitement. This was forbidden—it was lowborn—it was frighteningly different! She dipped two fingers into the rich plankton gravy, and then raised them to his mouth, just as Alceé had always done it for her. Her fingers felt weak and shaky, and her legs felt weak and shaky.

He opened his mouth, staring up at her in surprise. Did he guess her superior station, then? But then his mouth had closed over her fingers and his tongue was running down between them as she withdrew her hand. The effect was shocking. Her heart raced frantically as she dipped her fingers again into the food.

This time he seemed to know what to expect. His eyes were brown and liquid, and focused directly on hers. She felt a sense of communication rush between them, unlike anything she'd ever known. It was like a switch closing, somewhere inside her head, a circuit completed that had never been used before.

The door snicked open.

The gasp of guilt escaped her without her knowledge. Then she regained her control. *"You are a lady, My Miss Dorian. You will behave yourself as one at all times."* The voice inside her head was Albert's, and it had spoken to her many times.

The man in the doorway was her father. Behind him, face blank, was Wilma. "Well, then!" Damon said, his tone sharp and cutting. "Is *this* your station, Dorian?"

He had never before spoken to her like that. It was as if he had removed his gloves and whipped them across her face. (She'd seen him do that to someone only once. Shortly thereafter, he killed the man in a duel.)

When he questioned her, she answered quickly, quietly, aching to be done with it and flee.

"Very well, Dorian. You will go to my apartments, immediately. Wilma, you will do as you were originally instructed." He pointed to the door, and, shoulders slumping, she went out through it.

The gray mood was back.

18

Chapter Three

"YOUR NOVELTY ALONE IS OF no great value to us," Damon said. "It is true, you are unique. You are a living sample of our ancient history, which makes you a curiosity. But we are not interested in ancient history, and you are only a boy; you could know little even of your own barbaric age. Therefore, your only value to us lies in the fact that you are the first human being to be transported through time."

Frank felt himself split into two halves. What was it they said about being right-handed or left-handed? Right-handed people think with the left lobes of their brains, and vice-versa . . . and if you try to teach a left-handed person to be right-handed, all you do is to confuse his brain about which lobe, right or left, should dominate. So both try, and he stutters.

Could it be anything like this? Frank wondered. He seemed to hear with two ears, to understand with two brains. One half heard the tall man's speech as guttural syllables of noise—no more and no less so than the strange speech of these people had sounded to him earlier.

And the other half understood every word perfectly.

It was as if he'd been torn apart, split down the middle, into two people. One of them was the same Frank Marshall he'd always known himself to be: He spoke and understood only English (and two years of high-school French) and was the ordinary, maybe even dull, and slightly lonely product of what his Psych-Sociology teacher liked to refer to as "mid-century America."

But now he was also Frank Marshall, time-traveler, awake in a nightmare future where he could speak and understand an alien language. The sounds were at once right and very *wrong* in his ears, and his tongue twisted clumsily around the words as he automatically voiced them in reply.

"Th-through time?" he asked. "How far? I mean, when is this?" He was still on Earth, then—his surroundings were alien only in that they were those of another time.

When Damon answered him, the man's tone was caustic and condescending. "Young person, you are in what is for you the future. This is the year 501—or, umm, 24 . . . 58, Oldstyle."

Frank heard overtones in the tall man's voice and understood them. Damon had wrapped about him an air of smug superiority that obviously went unquestioned. He wore it as easily as he did his fringed blue cloak. "None of this," he told Frank, "excuses the licentiousness of your lowborn conduct with my daughter."

"I can't help that," Frank said. "I wasn't responsible for whatever it was your daughter was doing. In fact, I wasn't the one responsible for my being brought here in the first place. How am I supposed to know who you people are, or how you do things?" His breath was short and hard and he felt the tears of frustration welling up in him. How was he supposed to figure it all out before he even knew what was going on, anyway?

"It hardly matters; ignorance of the law is never an excuse," Damon replied coldly. "As for the responsibility for your being here, that is Manager Herron's. And shortly, I trust, he will be making repairs on the situation."

Damon thumbed the wall and a closet door slid neatly open. Inside was a white garment hanging limply from a hook. "Get dressed," he said. It was a dismissal. He did not nod or speak again. He simply left. The room's door closed shut behind him.

Frank sat on the bed, numbness washing over him in the wake of his bottled anger and frustration. He looked around without enthusiasm. The sun no longer shown in the window. The bright cheerfulness was gone; the room's colors were muted and overtoned with gray. *Why me?* he thought. *Why is this happening to me?*

Time-travel. The future. Science-fictional stuff. The Monster

20

from 2500 A.D., that sort of thing. Impossible. Straight from the comic books.

He climbed to his feet and lifted down the garment. It looked like a suit of long underwear, minus trapdoor. The front zipped up. It had its own built-in feet. It was very light.

So time-travel was impossible: Tell that to this Damon fellow. Something had sure yanked him, and a good-sized heap of his backyard, into this place, and if it wasn't time-travel, it was still unbelievable. So why did he believe it already?

The suit fitted snugly. A pair of boots stood on the closet floor. They too fitted. The garment was some kind of a jumpsuit. It fit almost like a second skin, and he didn't feel much less naked in it than he had before. But it was better than nothing; being naked among strangers in a strange place didn't leave a guy much room for carrying his self-confidence. It was a little too much like those uncomfortable dreams where he was undressed among fully-dressed people and out on the middle of a sidewalk—one of *those* dreams. "Anxiety dreams," the school psychologist had called them. "Everybody gets them at times. This is a trying period of your life, Frank." If he only knew how trying!

Damon seemed to be in charge around here—wherever *here* might be—and the girl, Dorian, was his daughter. She'd done something wrong in feeding him. Just as a guess, could it be that she wasn't supposed to use her fingers? But then again it was okay for the older woman in black. Didn't they have knives, forks, or spoons anymore? Didn't anybody feed himself? The people here were weirder than the place. . . .

The door opened.

Three men in silvery jumpsuits stood just outside. They were all tall and muscular-looking; they could've been stamped from a common mold. They looked like marines—or cops.

"Good, he's dressed," said one.

"You," said another, gesturing. "You understand me?" He spoke as if to a child, loudly and emphasizing each word.

Frank nodded. "I hear you," he said.

"Okay," said the first. "That's okay."

"You will come with us," said the second.

"All right," Frank said.

The third man—the one who had remained silent—seized

21

his arm, and propelled him forward at a fast march, down the corridor.

"Hey," Frank said. "Let up! You're hurting me. You don't have to do that!"

The man only grunted.

"You will not speak unless spoken to, parg," said one of the others from behind him. The word, "parg," did not immediately translate itself. It took him until they'd hustled him into an elevator to grasp its connotations: serf, peasant, filth-ridden scum—and more.

If the corridor outside his room had been attractively decorated in hues of iridescent floor tiles and glowing panels overhead, this elevator was its antithesis. It was bare, grim, and functional. It had all the feel of a freight elevator. Big, floor worn, wall-finish scratched, doors on two sides. It dropped like a stone, leaving his stomach and his breath back up on the floor above; then it shuddered to a stop so quickly that before they could catch up to him, it felt like they'd plummeted past.

The palace of the Heirs of Syncom is built atop a mountain in the Himalayas. Here the air is still relatively clean—clean enough that the snow that lies here year round is not soiled by the fallout of dirt as it is in other parts of the world, for instance—but too thin to be easily breathed without the aid of a respirator.

The palace itself is a tapering needle that stands thirty stories high, and sinks half a mile deep, within the mountain itself. Only the personal apartments and guest apartment of the Heirs—as well as a few auxiliary rooms such as that in which Frank Marshall awoke—are located within the tower portion. The remainder of the palace is sunken within the foundations of the mountain, and descends without pause into the great shops of the Syncom Corporation itself. The Grand Level is the uppermost of the buried portion of the palace; beneath it lie the servants' quarters, the kitchens, hydroponic gardens, clothing shops, and all the other personal industries necessary for the well-being of the Heirs. Yet farther down are some of those shops from which Syncom earns its standing and prestige as the greatest corporation in the System.

These shops are not the literal foundations of Syncom; they are research and development areas, as well as those places where necessarily controlled work can be handled. The invisible net of

22

Syncom reaches far beyond this single mountain, beyond, in fact, the planet Earth. Syncom is an amalgamation of corporations, growing originally from the semipublic corporation set up in 2013 (Old-style) to handle off-planet communications. Since then, Syncom has grown, like an immortal octopus, reaching and growing new arms in every direction which has presented itself and is not too heavily contested. Syncom owns refractories on Mars and Titan, all of the laser-relay stations beyond Earth's orbit, and has extensive holdings on the moon. In truth, Syncom's off-world holdings are far more extensive than those it has on Earth. This is at once its strength and its weakness.

Frank recognized the room. Its lights were still focused brightly on the heap of dirt that lay in the center of the large open floor. Half-shadowed machines stood at the edges of the pool of light, men moving in alien ritual among them.

They took him around the outer edge of the room and through another door. This was a smaller room. Like the larger, its walls were bare and functional. It appeared to be an office of some sort. In the center was a cluttered desk. To one side of the desk was something that looked very much like a computer outlet, complete with keyboard and print-out mechanism. To the other side of the desk was a chair. It looked like an oversized barber's chair. Wires ran from it to a machine that stood on a wheeled cart. The machine, white-enameled and knobby, appeared to be the first cousin to the machine from which he'd learned the language of the place. Both chair and machine were crowded into the room and obviously recent additions. Behind the desk, a man looked up.

Manager Herron. Frank didn't need to be told; he *knew.* There were still circles under Herron's eyes, but these were no longer caused by the goggle rims. They were the dark signs of sleeplessness. And when he looked up at Frank, Herron did so with eyes red-rimmed and bloodshot. His face was oily. He had the look of a man driven long past normal endurance. His expression was cold and distant.

"The boy, yes. He's ready?"

They handled him, Frank thought, like a piece of their hardware. They stripped him and wired him and plugged him in, these efficient labmen, just as they might prepare and fit a circuit module for a machine. In his case, they installed him in the chair. He was fastened so firmly that he couldn't even move.

Then they re-created for him in loving detail every moment, every instant, between the split seconds of his transition from *then* —August 2, 1969—to *now*. It was a little like the machine that had taught him their language, but this one did not *put in*. It *took out*.

He didn't lose consciousness. Instead, it was as if a switch had somewhere been thrown, stopping the forward movement of experience for him, and quickly reversing it, so that it might be played again, like a videotape recording, this time at half speed, in slow motion. What had taken so little time that he had felt it only as a blink of his eye, was stretched out into a seeming eternity that dragged by almost endlessly.

It was his unconscious mind they were restimulating: the physical memory synapses and neurons of the brain. Everything he ever thought, felt, or sensed was recorded in the molecular memory banks of his brain cells; everything that was *Frank Marshall* from the day he was born (and perhaps even, as some suggest, from before) was locked into chains of protein. Complete memories: total recall. The conscious mind can rarely touch them. But the labmen, the techs of Syncom, plugged directly into them. As if sorting through reels of tape, fitting one to a playback machine, hunting for the proper spot on it, and then playing and replaying it over and over, each time more slowly, more carefully, more exactingly, the labmen *played* Frank Marshall's memories of his hop through time.

It took two hours, four ounces of sweat, a thousand calories of expended energy, and every last detail recorded in his memories of that fleeting moment.

They ran him through it again and again. At first he tried to talk to them. He volunteered details, eager to cooperate. Finally, patient no longer, Herron pointed a finger at him and said, "Shut your mouth and be silent, or it will be fastened shut." Then he realized they were taking their readings from the machine, and analyzing them through the computer. They were recording him, recording his mind. They cared not at all for anything he might tell them.

And after that he shut up.

When they unplugged him, he felt very close to being a

24

vegetable. His mind was as limp as his body. He wondered, in that distant part of his mind that made it its business to wonder such things, if what they had done to him was anything at all like what doctors used to do to violent mental patients: they'd called it a shock treatment.

He did as he was told. When they told him to stand and dress himself, he tried. And when, after they roughly dressed him themselves, they told him to try walking, he tried. He did make his feet move when the two men took his arms, and it was close to walking. He even smiled a little in pleasure at the simple thought: *It's pretty close to walking.*

Behind him, he heard Manager Herron speak briefly. No one else was there, and he wondered at first if Manager Herron was speaking to him. After he'd heard what the man said, he decided Manager Herron was not speaking to him after all. It was probably to someone else. Maybe there was a telephone—or whatever passed for a telephone—here.

"No, sir," Herron had said. "About all we have is a solid date. And we already had that chalked in. Nothing else useful. The boy is a cipher, useless. We couldn't get any less out of the flagstones. . . . Yes, I hadn't expected better. . . . Yes, sir. He's fully expendable now; whatever you want done with him. I'm having him returned to his room."

Well, it didn't surprise Frank, either. What could you expect? He'd just been an innocent bystander, grabbed by accident. What could he possibly know that would help them? What was it they thought he'd know?

The knowledge that he was "fully expendable now" wormed around through his mind like a cold and deadly snake, and he knew it ought to bother him.

But it didn't. Not now. Not yet. He just felt like a happy vegetable.

Chapter Four

"WHAT ARE THEY GOING TO do with him?" Dorian asked. "The boy from the past, I mean. He's so young."

Albert leaned back in his chair. He always sat in the most comfortable chair in Dorian's sitting room. And whenever possible, he sat. He chuckled. "Not so young as you, though."

"You didn't answer my question."

"Dorian, you amaze me! Dear child, you have been strongly reprimanded by your father, you have been restricted to your quarters for a week, and you are in temporary disgrace, all because of your foolishness about this lowborn boy. And now, you can think of nothing but to ask after him!" He shook his head. "You are a most willful child. It was my fault you got into this. And now you want me to speak of him further? If you have no shame, think at least of your old tutor, whose hair is white and whose remaining years are few. Do you wish to see me cast out into the rubble-heap of discarded humanity at the foot of this mountain? Have you no consideration at all for your humble elders, child?"

For all of her impatience with him, she couldn't keep from bursting out laughing. "Oh, Albert! You know I wouldn't let anything like that happen to you! But still, I can't help being curious. Aren't you curious?" It was time for a flanking attack, she decided. The frontal assault had proved useless.

"Curious? About a person from the past? Oh, most assuredly. I'd love to have tapes of his memories. What a boon to historians! Imagine—all the minutiae of his daily life to sift through for the habit-patterns, folkways, and mores of his era! Ah, indeed yes. . . ." The old man's voice broke off in a ruminative sigh.

"Do you think they'll give you the chance?" Dorian asked, her voice ingenuous.

Albert shook his head. "I have my doubts. They recorded all he knew about the temporal transition, but nothing more. They are, as they say, 'men of science.' The cultural, the anthropological, the historical values are beyond them. Why, for all we know this boy may have attended an entertainment and seen the legendary Shakespeare himself!"

"Well, if they're finished with him," Dorian suggested, "why don't you see if you can have access to him for yourself?"

"I tried," the old man said. He shook his head wearily. "I am afraid, my dear, that I have shared your fall from grace with My Lord Damon. He was quite short on the subject. He gave me a flat no."

"Oh."

"Which does not, of course, answer your question. In point of fact, I do not know what they intend to do with him, but I suspect that whatever it is, it will be done rather soon now. His usefulness is ended to them. He is the product of an unfortunate accident, an experiment gone awry. He is only in the way, now." His eyes, as they peered up from under his bushy white brows, were piercingly direct, and they seemed to be telling her something. "I don't think there's much time left," Albert said. "Not for the boy."

Her heart seized, and she fought for a breath.

"Oh," she said. "Oh, I see."

27

Chapter Five

It wasn't like the movies.

He lay flat on his back on the eagerly hospitable bed. He felt as if he'd been put through a wringer. Like on an old-fashioned washing machine. Rolled flat.

In the movies time-travelers were given the keys to the city, at the very least! They got the guided tour and all the rest. And when the mayor's young and beautiful daughter fell in love with them, there was a beautiful romance, and then they took a prestigious job lecturing on the period they'd come from.

His mind ached. That was a funny way to put it, but it was true. Not a headache—a mindache. If he let his thoughts pick their own channels, it wasn't so bad. But if he tried to direct his thinking —toward what had really happened, or the way he was being treated, say—then the ache began to throb with every pulse beat, and his thoughts would grow confused, and he might even forget where he was or even *who* he was.

In the movies you were always *Somebody*. If an accident threw you into the future, it made a Somebody out of you. You were a celebrity, one of the Instantly Famous. People wanted to meet you, just to look at you, talk to you. The world in the movies was wide screen and technicolor, full of laughing happy people. . . .

. . . When he was thirteen, and took Ann Linbaugh to see *Doctor No* at the State, he'd tried to put his arm around her. It was the first time he'd tried it, but he knew it was standard operating procedure for a date at the movies. He'd raised his right hand and scratched his ear. Then he let it fall across the back of her seat. The seat was one of those old, old movie theatre seats—a curved wooden back with felt-plush upholstery. His arm lay on the narrow wooden edge along the top of the seat back. It was much too high. Her shoulders were at least two inches lower. She was wearing a sweater with a turtleneck. Her hair was long and pulled back in a ponytail. The ponytail tickled his arm when she moved. The action of the screen was very fast, not easily followed if you weren't paying close attention.

There was no way to get his arm down off that seat and around her shoulders: none at all. The movie made less and less sense to him. His cheeks grew progressively hotter. His arm began to ache. Then it went numb.

Finally he contrived to stretch, and managed to get his right hand back in his lap again. His right shoulder had a crick in it all night, and he couldn't sleep on it at all.

What a crush he'd had on that girl! Her parents moved a year later. Wonder what ever happened to her . . . ?

Tears filled his eyes. *It was so stupid!*

Mr. Yost was forever bawling him out in gym class.

"Marshall, get the lead outta your pants! Every boy in this class can stand on his head now; why can't you?"

He'd tried to explain it: "I dunno, Mr. Yost. I just can't get it. I keep falling over!"

And when he'd made a deal with Mr. Dee in science class, to help clean up after lab work and skip gym and phys-ed, his final quarter grade on phys-ed went from a D- up to a C. *That sure made a lot of sense!*

Mr. Helpern, the school psychologist: They'd sent him to see Mr. Helpern so often it was a joke. "I'm getting extra credits in sociology class," he'd say, just to turn the bitter joke first. "I'm studyin' to be a nut."

"You just don't have the proper attitude, Frank," Mr. Helpern would say. "If you want to get into college, you must cultivate the proper attitude. This is an adult world you're entering. You must leave your childhood behind you. You must develop a sense of responsibility for yourself. Now, take a look at your grades for the last quarter. . . ."

They were always pushing. They tried to push you right through childhood just as fast as they could. It was as if grown-ups resented your being a child. He still remembered the sullen anger he'd felt when his mother had told him, "No, Frank, I'm not going to help you dress anymore. You're four years old now, and you're old enough to dress yourself."

Or Mrs. Woods, his fifth-grade teacher: "Frank, I don't want to see you carrying on like that during recess. Little Teddy Edwards lost his glasses in that scuffle."

"But, ma'am, we were just chicken-fighting. And it was pure accident Teddy's glasses got knocked off. He was on *my* back; I was carrying him. He was with *me*. *I* didn't want to see his glasses get busted!"

"Frank, you're the biggest boy in my class, and you're the oldest. In fact, I don't mind telling you, you're the brightest. I insisted on it, in fact. I wanted them to leave me one of the brighter boys to set an example for the class." So that's why he was in that dull woman's slow class! He'd wanted to hit her when she'd told him that.

"Now, it's up to you to set the proper example for the younger children, the smaller children in class. I don't want to see any more of this, ahh, 'chicken-fighting' during recess. If you've got a lot of excess energy to burn off, I suggest you do calisthenics on the bars.

"Frank, you have a responsibility to yourself, you know. You must act your age."

They never let you be a child. They were always pushing at you to grow up, just as fast as possible. They dinned it into you: *Responsibility,* act your age, *grow up,* don't be an underachiever, *you must cultivate the proper attitude . . . !*

So, what good was it all now?

The tears squeezed out and rolled down his cheeks and into his ears. It was all so suddenly long ago and far away. . . .

Oh, God, he felt so lonely.

The light from the opening door jarred him awake. The room

was dark. The light was a bright square that outlined a figure. He blinked his eyes, then knuckled them. Someone stood silhouetted in the doorway, staring at him.

A hand fumbled the wall, and then the ceiling began to glow. It was a soft glow, warm and not too bright. The door closed. It was the girl—Dorian.

He sat up. "What are you doing here?" he whispered. An old movie cliché struck him: *The walls have ears.* He wondered if they did, here.

"Are you all right?" she asked. It was a kind of dumb question, really. How could he answer a question like that?

She touched the wall again, and the overhead light grew dimmer. It seemed to take on her conspiratorial mood. She was wearing robes of rich brown tonight, the edges all in fur. She motioned him back up the bed until he was sitting with his back against the low headboard. The bed readjusted itself around him. She sat down at the foot and leaned forward.

"Tell me: What was it like, back in your age?" she asked. Her voice was soft-pitched, as if she too was afraid of being overheard.

He still didn't feel quite awake, quite human. He shook his head. "My age . . . ?" he mumbled. His tongue was fuzzy.

"I mean, what was the world like, then? Did your people wear clothes? Did they make fires, or anything like that?"

"You're kidding," he said, giving her a sharper look. "You're putting me on. It's only been five hundred years, you know."

"What's that mean? 'Putting me on'?" Her expression was open, the question innocent.

He felt a sudden unreasoning stab of irritation. "Look, suppose you tell *me*. All I've seen around this place is this room, a lot of hallways, and the dungeon. Where am I, anyway? And," he asked, something cold forming itself into a ball in his gut, because he'd already guessed the answer, "what are they going to do with me?"

Her expression became grave. "I don't know," she said.

She knew. She knew something, anyway.

"You came to sight-see?" he asked, bitterly. "Big novelty, folks—a real, honest-to-God time-traveler! He's right here, in our big tent, for a limited time only! See him while ya' can; he won't be here much longer! Hurry, hurry, hurry! That's right, lady, you can pinch his toe, 'cause he's real, he's alive, he breathes, he walks, he talks! He does everything except make it. He's a little sullen, folks, just a little moody, but don't you pay him no mind for that, because to*mar*raw we're gonna replace him with a giant ape that does handstands!" Frank's low voice was sardonically satirical.

"Please," Dorian said. "Please, don't talk like that."

"What would happen if your father found out you were here?"

"He'd—but he won't. He can't. Nobody knows I'm here, nobody knows I came here this time. Last time Wilma told him, but she doesn't know now."

"Are you all excited? Big thrill, forbidden adventure, all that?" he asked cynically.

"Yes," she said. "I guess so." She looked very much a little girl, pretty and innocent, thrust into a situation too deep for her to understand. He knew he was trying to hurt her. He wondered why. "Nothing like you ever happened here before."

"Goody, goody."

"You don't like me?" she asked. "You don't want to talk to me?"

He'd succeeded. No one had ever spoken to her this way before. No one had ever tried to hurt her like this.

"Your father'll have another fit, if he finds out you've been here again—with a, uh, *parg."* He couldn't let it up; he couldn't stop. What was he trying to do? Get at the father through his daughter?

"You're *not!* People aren't supposed to *say* words like that, you know. But you're not a, what-you-said. Wilma would never have fed you. It would be disgusting." She was struggling to hold on, now.

"Look, Dorian," he said, sitting up straighter. "Let's square it away, okay? Last time you were here, your father took it out on me. At first they had pretty decent treatment lined up for me— a decent bed, food, clothing at least. Since all that fuss about you, I've been shoved around, had my mind wired for sound, and been just generally treated like dirt—like a parg, whatever it is. And, let's not forget something: I'm just a dumb barbarian. I wouldn't know people aren't supposed to use words like that. After all, it got used on *me.*

"So, anyway: What are you doing here now? What's going to happen to me *this* time? That's what I'm asking myself. All I see is a girl whose father pulls a lot of weight, who's come to the zoo to see the funny monkey from the past. That's all I am to you, that's all you are to me.

"Now you know, and I know it too, I'm not slated to be around much longer. If I was, you wouldn't be sneaking in here late at night like this, for your last big look. I dunno what they have in mind for me, and maybe you don't know exactly, either. But we can both guess, and I don't really think they're gonna send me back where I came from. Not this soon. I was just a freak accident, and they're about to bury this accident.

"So you tell me this: Why should I be so happy to see you now? Why should I want to talk to you? Huh?"

It stopped her. It stopped her cold. It was easy to see. She looked as though he'd hit her, as if he'd slapped her with the back of his hand. She was staring down at the bed, her head bowed, and her fingers were picking aimlessly, nervously, at an edging of fur. Little brown hairs were scattered all over on the white sheet of the bed.

When she looked up, it was with something in her moist eyes he couldn't read: Fear? Sorrow? Contrition?

Her voice was small and very young. "I'm—sorry. I . . . I guess I don't know very much. I didn't think. That's what Albert is always telling me: I don't think." She put her hands down on the bed and pushed herself back off it and onto her feet. She turned with slumped shoulders for the door.

"Hey," he said. He felt real cold and distant, and his voice came out funny. The sight of her defeat brought him no joy at all. The malice he'd felt toward her was suddenly gone. It had turned into a lump of ice. "Wait a minute. Don't go away yet. Please."

When she turned back something glistened on her cheek for a moment. It made something twist inside him. His head felt light, and he knew he had no control over himself—no control over what he was saying and doing. That was wrong.

"Look," he said. "I, umm, I guess I shouldn't have said all those things. You, uhh, you're the only person here who's really tried to talk to me." *It wasn't right to take it all out on her.*

She came back to the bed and sat down shyly on one corner of it.

"Why don't we swap?" Frank said. "I'll tell you about where

I came from, and you tell me about this place. Okay? And . . . you're sure nobody will miss you, wherever you're supposed to be?"

She shook her head in answer to his last question. "I'm supposed to be asleep," she said. Her face lit for a moment with the sharing of the secret. "They think I'm locked up in my apartment."

"It's a deal, then?" he asked.

"All right," she said. She smiled. "It's a deal."

"—I bought my first car when I was sixteen," Frank said. "A '59 Ford Galaxy. Lots of chrome, real smooth looks—I paid a hundred dollars for it, and I really thought I had something. I didn't put five thousand miles on it before it threw a rod and blew the engine."

"—I don't understand," Dorian said. "If your father worked for a government, why wasn't he a drone?"

"—I decided I wanted a sports car, so I tapped some of my college savings and invested in a Jaguar. I had to get a job afternoons, after school, to make the payments. Beautiful little thing, a coupé, XK 120. It was perfect for dates, because it only had two seats and you never had to worry about third parties. But when summer came, every time I stopped for a red light it would boil over. I guess my problem is, I get sold on the *looks* of a car, and I don't pay enough attention to the guts inside. Besides which, it wouldn't even pass inspection. Big sports-car company sold it to me, Manhattan Auto, they even sponsored races. But they'd put in an illegal exhaust system, and it wouldn't pass Virginia's state inspection."

"—Governments are just for drones and the lowborn, anyway. Everybody knows they don't really *do* anything. We Heirs are the ones who really make things run. That's what I'm being trained for. Some day I'll be important, and I'll stand behind my husband while he holds audiences with his managers."

"—Dad was in civil service; that's not like being in politics or anything. As a matter of fact, you're not supposed to make any public statements on political issues if you're in civil service, although I guess some people do. Dad worked for the Bureau of Agriculture. Two or three times a year, they'd send him out on field trips. Usually he couldn't take us along, but one year he took me with him—

I was fifteen—and I saw the Midwest and the West. We took a plane to Chicago, and then trains from there. Dad says there aren't any trains in the East worth using. But you really get the feel of the country when you go through it by train. In a plane it just looks all flattened out and covered with clouds."

"—I've been raised to be an Heir. You don't know how important that is. Correct behavior requires correct thinking. My tutor says the lowborn never learn to really think, not the way an Heir must. What's a 'date'?"

Communication was difficult. They had few common grounds upon which to meet. Frank tried to tell Dorian about the way in which he'd lived, the school he'd gone to, what his parents did. He tried to tell her that in his day government was not a figurehead—not so much anyway—for the big corporations that really tried to run things. Politics was a meaningless idea to her—everyone in government, as far as she was concerned, must be a drone, a nobody who did nothing but look quite elegantly as if he was indeed a somebody who did something—window dressing for the lowborn.

The concept of separate nations was also lost on her; he found that out when he wondered aloud if she meant something like England's constitutional monarchy: the idea of a king or queen who did not truly govern, but in whose name the government acted.

Dorian was a sheltered, isolated member of her own world. Raised from infancy in this vast, sprawling palace, she had never in her life stepped outside it. What she knew of the world beyond was what she had been taught or had gleaned from others. She was being trained to take her place in the society of Heirs—that and little more. Her world view was narrow, parochial, and incredibly chauvinistic.

Nevertheless, Frank began to slowly piece together a picture of the world of the future in which he found himself.

It was not a pleasant picture, but somehow he hadn't expected it would be. It was a world ruled by a hereditary elite: the Heirs of the great and minor corporations. It was a greatly class-conscious society, and it was spread planet-wide, even system-wide.

There were, theoretically, only three classes. At the bottom were the serfs, the lower class. They lived amid almost overwhelming population pressures, at the bottoms of the canyons of the world's cities, rarely ever even aware of the light of day. Dorian knew little about them, and cared even less. They were the sediment of society, settled out upon the world's floor, fit only for walking over—or "trodding upon," as Frank's mind rephrased it in English as the tired cliché popped into his mind.

At the top were the Heirs. Like Dorian. At some time in the distant past, the forerunners of the Heirs had consolidated their corporate wealth into a family structure. Perhaps it began with John D. Rockefeller, the Elder. Or perhaps Henry Ford, Senior. Or maybe James V. Ling. Or Harvey Eisenberg, who was the first to take private enterprise to other planets with the company whose seed when planted became, eventually, Syncom.

Money breeds money; power breeds power. Fathers passed their wealth and holdings to their sons. Dynasties developed.

At some point the heirs became the Heirs, titled nobility of the most practical sort: those who would wield the world's greatest power structures—the great corporations.

Between these two class extremes was the gulf. It was considered the middle class. Everyone else fit into it, willy-nilly. It was theoretically possible for anyone, even those most lowborn, to rise high in the middle class, possibly even into high managerial positions within the corporations, on the basis of ability alone. In fact, that was supposed to be the test. It was, Dorian explained, the highest form of democracy. Those in the bottom class were there because they were unfit for better: They had failed every test of life. Each man was free to find his own level—barring that of the top, of course—as best he could. For her the whole world and everything beyond it was only a dim reflection of the reality here at home. She missed nothing, wanted for nothing.

"And, when I am eighteen I shall marry Elton."

"Eighteen? How old are you now?"

"Sixteen; almost seventeen, really. I'll be seventeen in three weeks. Elton will be at my birthday ball. I haven't seen him for a year, now."

"Why? I mean, if you're engaged to marry the guy . . . ?"

"I only see Elton on corporate occasions, and, now, at my birthday balls. He's Transystems, you see—Heir Apparent—and he only comes here at special invitation. My father says that even that's too often, but my tutor, Albert, he says that's just natural corporate hostility speaking."

"Let me get this straight, now. This guy Elton belongs to a different corporation? And his corporation rivals yours? But you're marrying him? Don't your parents object?"

"Why should they?" she replied. "They picked him for me. I've been pledged to Elton ever since the day I was born."

It was at that point that the lights went out.

Chapter Six

DORIAN SQUEALED. THEN HE FELT the bed reshape itself as she leaped to her feet. Her hands made slapping sounds on the wall.

"What's happened?" he asked. "What happened to the lights?"

"I don't know, I don't know," she wailed. "I can't get them back on. And—I'm afraid of the dark."

"Open the door to the hall," he said, getting off the bed. His right hand touched the smooth glass of the window. He bent his head and peered out.

"I—I *can't,*" Dorian said. "It won't open! Nothing works!"

There was no moon, but the snow below glowed in the faint starlight. No lights shone brightly on it from the palace tower. That could only mean that all the lights were off! A power failure?

Dorian's groping fingers grazed against his back, and he jumped, startled.

"Oh!" she said. "Is something happening—outside?"

He grabbed her hand so it would stay put and not surprise him again. He stared out again. He started to shake his head, then paused. Something moving—a shadow?

A black object, a round blot against the stars, maybe very small and close, maybe big and faraway, was getting bigger, closer. Then—

"Back!" Frank shouted, knocking Dorian onto the floor and falling over her.

It all happened at once:

There was the sound of shattering glass *and*—

There was a shrill whistle of escaping air that dropped like a roller coaster into a deep bass *whoosh, and*—

Frank's ears popped as he swallowed and popped again *and*—

Numbing cold filled the room with icy fingers *and*—

Dorian screamed *and*—

He gasped for breath, the thin cold air like sharp knives in his throat, his lungs heaving with panic, *and*—

He could no longer see what was happening at the windows; black spots and brilliant exploding sparks of light filled his eyes *and*—

He lost consciousness.

His head was splitting. His mouth felt swollen and dry, and when he tried to wet his lips, he tasted bile on them.

He was wrapped in a cocoon, or maybe a straitjacket. Something soft and clinging held him in a tight bundle so he couldn't move. It was completely black. All he could see were the stars he made by squeezing his eyes too tight. Fabric lay against the skin of his hands and his face. It tickled his nose, but his stomach was too queasy to allow a sneeze. It rubbed against his chin, chaffed against his neck. The air he breathed was hot and close, but he *could* breathe. His hands were bound at his sides, and he could barely wriggle one finger. He was lying on his back on something hard. The surface under him was vibrating. It didn't help his pounding headache, nor his nausea. He hoped he wouldn't get sick. He didn't even want to think about how messy it would be if he did.

The surface under him inclined suddenly to one side, and something heavy but soft was pitched against him. He heard a muffled groan. It cut through the drumming of his pulse in his ears and the other sounds which might be engine noises.

"Dorian?" he said, pitching his voice as low as he could. He couldn't turn his head in her direction.

"Frank?" came her distant, muffled reply.

"What happened?" he asked.

"I don't know. Don't you know?"

39

It hurt to talk. Moving his chin made the cloth tighten on his throat and made him gag. "No," he said.

"Oh," she said. She didn't say anything else. He wondered if she felt sick, too.

The surface tilted again, the other way. The vibrations increased in pitch. He felt her body lying beside his, and felt strangely comforted. At least she was with him; he wasn't completely alone.

He didn't think he could possibly fall asleep with the vibrations jarring his head like that, but he did, anyway. Because when the vibrations stopped, the sudden cessation startled him awake.

He heard a metallic *clang* and felt it the same moment through the surface on which he was lying. His ears felt the pressure adjustment, and he swallowed. His mouth tasted dry and awful.

"Dorian?" he called.

"What in blazes—?" said a sudden voice from somewhere overhead and very close. "There's two of 'em here!"

"Ah, yessir," came a voice from further away. "That's what there was, sir. Two of 'em."

"Orders were to pick up a boy," snapped the first voice. "Just one boy." Frank felt hands grab him and wrest him up into a sitting position. The cloth wrap cut like a steel band across his belly, and in the cramping spasm of nausea he lost the next exchange.

". . . but we had the right room—number K-11 on the plans —and there was two of them in there . . ." the second voice was saying.

"So you picked up both," finished the first voice.

"Orders were, the occupant of the room. Well, now, they was both occupying the room, wasn't they?"

"Maxwell, if you've bungled this like I think you have, you'll be happy just to lose both hands," said the first voice from very close to Frank's right ear. Hands were tugging at him, doing something. Then—

The cloth parted from his face and he could see. A big man with a dark blue uniform was stooping at his side. The room was small and metal-walled. Bright light from a single overhead lamp glared harshly on a second figure blocking the open door.

"Okay, this is the right one, all right," said the man next to him.

"What'd I tell you, huh? I told you we got him."

40

"Yes, you pargson, and would you like to wager on the second one?"

"Huh?"

Frank turned his head to watch as the big man pulled a mummy-like figure, swathed in brown cloth, to a sitting position. The man unwrapped the mummy's head, and Dorian blinked her eyes.

"Well, Maxwell, you did it," the big man said. "You really did it this time. You have just successfully kidnapped the daughter of the Heir of Syncom."

The man in the doorway moved quickly into the room, his breath expelled in a sudden wordless exclamation. "No! Naw, I couldn't have! I mean, what would *she*—?"

The other backhanded him across the mouth. Maxwell staggered, then raised his hand to touch his face.

"Just beautiful, Maxwell," the big man said. "Just absolutely beautiful. You just lost your head."

Maxwell turned white.

"I'm not scared," Dorian insisted. They sat facing each other, their backs against the opposite walls of the tiny room. "They'll let us go. They'll *have* to."

"Why?" Frank asked.

"Because of who I am. You heard the man. He recognized me. It's all some sort of awful mistake, and now they'll take care of it."

Frank glanced at the closed door. The two men had not been gone long. "It didn't sound like a mistake to me," he said. "That was a carefully planned raid. They knocked out the power, and then they came right through the window. They knew which window. They wanted my room. They wanted *me*."

"Yes, of course," Dorian said, her voice a little brittle. "But not me. That was a mistake. It was a bad mistake. Why, when Elton finds out about it . . ."

"Why Elton?"

"Didn't you see their insignia? The 'T' over diagonal? They're Transystems."

"You mean a rival corporation arranged this whole thing?"

"They must have found out about you," she said, nodding. "Naturally, they'd want to get you. So would any big corporation,

41

and Transystems is biggest next to Syncom." The pride in her voice struck Frank ironically.

"So all you have to do is clap your hands, and they'll send you back home," he said. "But what about me?"

"I don't know," she said, and suddenly her voice was small again. "I'm sorry, Frank."

"Well, I don't guess it's much worse than what I would've ended up with back there," Frank said, gloomily.

"I'm really sorry."

"Yeah, I know you are. So'm I." The self-pity loomed up black within him, and he felt its acid taste in his mouth. Frying pan to fire. Some luck.

When the door opened again, it was the big man, alone.

"Time to go, kiddies," he said. "Don't think it wasn't fun, because it wasn't."

"Where's Maxwell?" Frank asked.

"Better you shouldn't know; you'll be joining him soon enough."

"What's that mean?" Dorian asked. The man was doing something to the cloth that was wrapped around Frank's legs; Frank felt it suddenly go loose.

"Let's face it," the man said in reply. "There's got to be a better world to come, right? 'Cause this one's just too lousy to be the whole story."

The blood rushing back into Frank's legs set them into fiery agony. "What're you trying to say, mister?" he asked.

The man performed a similar task, freeing Dorian's legs. Then he lifted her to her feet. She tottered, but managed to keep stand-ing. The man didn't speak.

"What're you going to do with us?" Frank demanded. The man hoisted him up, and he tried to balance himself on his numb feet. His hands and arms were still bound. It was like being on stilts.

"You really want to know, I'm going to dump you," the man said. "I got the dirty duty to clean up after the late Maxwell, is what it is, and I don't much care for it more'n you do, but I aim to keep my own head on my shoulders. Getting my brain wired into an organic computer circuit is not my idea of the best way to spend the next life."

Dorian swayed. "You're—going—to—*kill*—us?"

He put a hand on each of them, and guided them through the door. They were in a corridor, with windows along its side. Through the windows Frank caught glimpses of a flat sun-washed deck, across which strange vehicles sped before arcing up into the sky. Airport?

"You lucked out, that's all," the man said, as he hustled them down the narrow corridor past closed doors. "Bad luck all around. Bad accident, gotta clean it up fast."

"But I'm Dorian, of Syncom!" Dorian said, her voice caught between haughtiness and pleading. "You can't do that!"

"I guess you're wrong," the man said. They entered a square room. The floor began to drop, carrying them down two levels. "I guess I will."

"But, but *why?*" she asked.

"Wrong time, wrong place, looks like," the man said. Now they were heading back along another corridor. At its end, a door stood open. "You've seen too much, you know too much. It would embarrass the Heirs, I guess. It's better nobody sees, nobody knows."

"But I'm to marry Elton. When he finds out—"

"He won't. The Old Man made the decision on this personally. He's not going to spread it around. I took Maxwell to him myself. Far's I know, it's between just him and me, now."

"The 'Old Man'?" Dorian exclaimed. "Elton's *father?*"

"So what's going to happen to *you?*" Frank asked. "Once you've taken care of us, why should *you* know?"

The door led into a hangar-like room, several levels high and tapering at its far end. Several helicopter-like machines stood on its floor. One stood free of guy-wires, its blades turning lazily. Its body was a fat bug, mouth an open ramp. The man pushed them up the ramp and into the copter. It was impossible to resist; it was difficult to even walk. Only their calves were freed; their thighs were still bound together. Walking was like the mincing steps of women in too-tight dresses. It made Frank feel peculiarly helpless and humiliated. He didn't dwell on it. He was too scared, too unwilling to let it all end, like this, so emptily. . . .

Dorian grunted when the man shoved Frank over onto her. They lay in a heap on the copter's bare metal floor, just behind the pilot's seat.

43

"Why should he stop with you?" Frank asked again. His heart was hammering, and his teeth wanted to chatter, but he tried to hold his voice steady. "Why share it with you, huh?"

The man shook his head; his ear loop swung back and forth. He didn't turn around to look at them. "I do my job, I get by," he said. "I wasn't stupid. I knew enough to take it to the top. With luck, I'll get a promotion."

Big doors opened in the side of the hangar, and the man began manipulating his controls. The copter engines built up into a turbine whine, and then the copter was rolling toward the doors. The overhead blades began to turn faster, their *thwopping* rhythm accelerating into a steady thumming.

The copter lifted, tilted a little, and shot quickly and easily out into the open. For a moment the pilot held the copter in a motionless hover, and Frank caught his first and last sight of the great whale of a craft from whose stomach they had just emerged. It was shaped like a huge blunt cigar, tiers of thin swept-back wings along its fusilage, tiny and ridiculous looking. Its engines were not visible. It looked like nothing Frank had ever seen before, even in the wildest comic book. Then the copter scooted high into the air and off at a sudden angle across the sky.

"How are you going to do it?" Frank asked. Thin wisps of clouds swept past the cockpit bubble, and beyond them were fluffy yellow billows and a dirty gray-blue sky.

"We'll be over open water in another few minutes," the man answered. "Then I'll dump you."

Dorian was sobbing softly.

"There must be another way," Frank said.

"Sure—lots. But you don't want to add your brains to a micromolecular computer circuit, do you? You don't want to be part of a protein communications system, right? So this way is fast and easy, and requires no witnesses."

"I mean, you shouldn't have to kill *her*. If she's all set to marry into your corporation anyway—?"

"If Maxwell hadn't pulled his trick, we wouldn't have to do this at all. But, buddy, you just don't understand. Transystems is a *nice* corporation. Transystems wouldn't kidnap Damon of Syncom's daughter. *Never*. And when word gets out, officially, I reckon young

44

Elton will send flowers and his official grief, and maybe even the Old Man will get on the direct circuit to present his deepest sympathies. You know?"

Dorian stifled her sobs. "Syncom would never do a thing like this."

The pilot's only reply was a mordant "Ho, ho, ho."

The turbines shrieked and the air whistled, and all too soon, the copter was slowing and gliding down, nose dipped so that Frank could just barely catch the glint of sunlight dancing on water through the front bubble.

"End of the line, kiddies," the pilot said.

"We'll be seeing you again," Frank said. "You know that."

The man's big shoulders shrugged. "Maybe. And then again, maybe not."

"If he'd have Dorian killed just so no one would know she'd been kidnapped by mistake, you think he'll leave you alive?" Frank asked. "You better think it through, mister." It was his only argument, but just maybe—if he could convince the big man it was the truth—

"Take us back to my father," Dorian spoke up, "and you'll live a lot longer."

The man laughed. "Back to your father? Halfway around the world? In this thing? Forget it."

At least he was willing to talk about it.

"You could find a way if you wanted to," Frank said.

"My father would reward you richly," Dorian said.

"Sure he would. And a Transystems assassin would take care of me in just days," the man replied. "Don't make it any harder on yourselves, huh? Stop begging."

"What's the matter?" Frank asked, bitterly. "Can't you take it, the sight of two kids begging for their lives? Are we supposed to go out grinning like fools or something? Would you?"

"It's just my job," the man said. "That's all it—"

The bottom of the copter dropped out from under them. Frank had one clear glimpse of the copter suddenly above them, bay-doors on its underside hanging open, flapping, the interior of the fat bug suddenly dark in the thick yellow sunshine. Then his body was twisting in the air, and he saw the blur of Dorian from the corner

45

of his eye. He was trussed like a mummy, helpless, and he couldn't even get his hand to his nose before he hit. He tried to straighten his legs—

—and suddenly smashed deep into the water, water green and dark in his eyes, bitter and stinging in his nose, stifling in its demand on his lungs. He was plunging down, down, deeper into the dark and roaring depths, and he sighed, bubbles rippling from his mouth up his face and before his staring eyes, and let himself go limp.

Chapter Seven

HER ROBES WERE TORN AND still heavy with water; the fur edgings were matted. The sun was a thin yellow in the yellowed sky; its heat disappeared with every gust of wind.

"Here, now!" the old man shouted. "You just stop that, now! You just stop even thinking such things!"

The ribbed plastic of the deck rose and fell beneath her stomach and she stayed sprawled full length upon it, as much for the security in lying pressed against it in these heaving seas as for any protection from the chilling wind.

"Come *on,* Pop," the thin gangling boy said. "Get *with* it. This is too good, too jes' fine!" He gestured with his right arm, but the arm ended at his wrist: he had no right hand.

Dorian felt unbearably sick. Her body shook with chills and her teeth chattered against each other. Each time the small boat crested a swell it seemed her stomach would rise into her throat and choke her. She squeezed her eyes shut and turned her head away from the sight of the skinny boy's handless stump and wide malicious grin, and opened them again to stare once more at the still unconscious figure of Frank Marshall soddenly stretched out on the deck beside her. He did not stir; she was trapped alone in this incredible nightmare.

"We saved their lives, Boy!" the old man was arguing angrily.

His red face was purpling and veins stood out, throbbing, at his temples. He wiped his mouth with the back of his hand. He had two hands. "What'd we do that for, I want to ask you, huh?"

"So we fished them out. Fine-o. Sure—that was before the girl started squeaking about who she was and all that. That was before we made it out they ain't people." The thin boy's voice was jauntily sardonic.

"I'm gonna whip you, Boy," the old man said. "You got a mouth on you, what you shouldn't have. 'Course they's people! What else could they be if they ain't people, answer me that!"

The boy spat. *"You* know damned well, Pop. They's Overmen—like the girl-brat says, they's *Heirs."* He pronounced it *hares.* "It's their kind what did *this* t'me!" He held up his right arm.

"Boy, Boy . . ." the old man said, his voice rumbling from deep inside his chest. "Now you was caught square-even on that, and it was Levi who shortened your arm, not no Overmen." He chuckled. "Told you yore fingers was too highborn for you. . . ."

The body lying next to her groaned, and for a moment Dorian was not convinced the sound had not been her own. Then she felt a cold hand brush wetly against her arm.

The touch sent a sudden chill racing through her and she flinched away from it, biting her lip at the same moment. Suddenly Frank Marshall's eyes opened, and he was staring directly into hers.

Her heart seemed to seize while violently opposed reactions fought themselves inside of her: He was awake—that was good! *She hated to be touched.* He was looking right *at* her—but his eyes seemed unfocused. . . .

"Oh, God, I feel awful," he said, but the words were English, and they meant nothing to her.

"Frank," she said, her voice low but urgent. "You've got to wake up! It's important."

He groaned again, and then he recognized her. "Dorian," he whispered. The sound of her name froze her breath for a moment. "Thought we were drowned . . . dead. . . ."

She raised an arm to gesture at the old man and the skinny boy standing in the cockpit aft and above, still arguing between themselves. "They pulled us out; they rescued us."

She watched as he raised himself up on his elbows and directed his gaze upward. "They saved us?" he asked. He still seemed a little fuddled.

"Yes, and now they're arguing about us. The boy wants to throw us back into the water again."

He shook his head, then grimaced at her. "Back in again?" he repeated. "Why?"

"I don't know," she said, wishing she could be certain she did indeed not know. "I had only thanked them and told them how grateful my father would be. Then the boy just exploded at me!"

"Where'd they come from?" he asked.

"I don't know. I didn't see them—before, when I was falling, I mean. Maybe they were here all along."

"I thought sure I was dead," he said.

"They pulled me out first. The old man said he thought at first you *were* dead. You weren't breathing, you know." A shudder went through her at the memory, and then she was shivering again and her teeth chattering.

"They saved our lives, then?" he asked, "and now they want to throw us overboard again?"

"The boy. The old man is arguing with him. When I told the boy who I was, he gave me such a look that I knew instantly that he was full of hate for me." Then, quite before she'd known it would happen, she was blinded by salty tears that filled her eyes and ran quickly down her cheeks. She closed her eyes and squeezed them, hoping he hadn't seen. She didn't know why.

His nostrils burned and the back of his throat felt sand-papered with the aftertaste of the choking brine he'd swallowed. He felt very dizzy and very weak, and the knowledge that he was alive was in itself enough for him.

He kept his eyes open because when he'd let them close again blackness had swept over him like a lethargic blanket and he'd had to gasp a shuddering breath for fresh air. *It had been so easy to surrender.* The water had been so thick around him, and so numbingly cold. It was a memory he would never entirely forget; it would always haunt his worst dreams.

Dorian had her face buried against the deck and her shoulders were heaving—whether with sobs or shivers he couldn't tell. He raised

49

his arm to put it around her, but halted with the high-pitched laugh from overhead.

He looked up. The small boat's cockpit was a low bridge with a streamlined windscreen, the top of which was only three or four feet above the level of the deck. The skinny boy had his foot on the furled edge of the windscreen and was staring down at them with a twisted smile.

The boy leapt down onto the deck with the agility of a monkey, his bare feet sure on the wet corrugated plastic of the heaving deck. Frank rolled over on his back and pushed himself up to a sitting position.

"You," the boy said, thrusting his toe at Dorian. "Got any money?"

She pulled away from him, curling herself on her side to avoid him. "Money?" she asked blankly.

Frank watched the tableau silently, as though it was being played before him on a television screen.

The boy was leaning over Dorian while she hid her face from him. "Yeah, *money*. You know, the fist, your old man's clout, honey-girl."

"I don't have any money," came her muffled voice in tearful protest. "What would *I* do with it?"

The boy laughed. "You might buy your way free, know what I mean?"

"Free?" Dorian asked, uncovering her face.

"Oh, boy! Looka her, Pop! A real brain, huh? Real top-stuff, you betchum." He snorted. "Yeah, honey-girl: *free*. Like, alive and on land?"

"But I don't have any money," Dorian said. She raised a hand to brush back her short hair from her cheek. "I've never had any."

The boy threw back his head and laughed, and his laughter made chills run up and down Frank's spine. "She's never had any money! You hear that, Pop? She's never had any!" The boy doubled over with his manic laughter, tears flowing from his eyes.

Something thumped heavily on the deck behind him, and Frank half turned his head as the old man, short and barrel-shaped, shot out a meat-hook hand and grabbed the boy, pulling him up straight.

"Hey, now, Boy!" he spoke gruffly but strangely kind. "Watch yourself, Boy. You know where that leads you! 'Sides, what d'you know about them Overmen, huh? Maybe she's telling it right—din't have nothing on her when we hauled 'er out, did she, huh?"

It was time to say something. Frank opened his mouth and waited for a sound to come out. It took three tries. Then, "We were kidnapped," he said, his voice a sharp rasp in his sore throat. "We didn't have time to grab the family jewels."

He sensed Dorian's eyes on him, but didn't take his own attention away from the boy.

The boy began to laugh again, but when his eyes locked on Frank's, there was a crazy glint to them. "Now that one, he's jes' fine," he said, worming free of the old man's clutch.

"Hey, now," he said, dropping down to a squat before Frank. "Want to buy free? Huh? Want to do it, boy?"

Frank started to push himself back a little. This crazy kid bothered him. The thin boy reached out his stubbed right arm and pushed it against Frank's chest.

His arms gave, and he fell back flat. "I don't have any more money than she does," he said.

"Naw, I don't wantcha money, sonny-boy," the boy said. He was grinning, but his face was very tense, his lips drawn thin. "Gimme your right hand. Gimme your *hand,* fine one, and you're free."

A cold knife traced its way down Frank's spine and twisted itself into his stomach. *The boy was really mad!*

"My hand? You're crazy!"

The boy would've leaped on him, tooth and nail, elbows and knees, if the old man hadn't collared him again, his big hand clamping on the back of the boy's neck as if the boy was a kitten to be yanked out of the prize flower bed. The boy was making noises, mewling sounds, and spittle was rolling from his working lips. But the old man kept a firm grip on him, his bandied legs braced for the unending roll and pitch of the deck while he held the boy.

"You shouldn't'a said that, boy," the old man said to Frank. "That was just now the wrong thing to say."

Dorian was sitting up, her fluffy, frilly clothes clinging wetly around her. "But he *is,*" she said. "Why'd he talk like that? Why's he so mean?"

The old man lifted his fist and clouted the boy on the side

51

of his head, behind his ear. "Only way to calm him down," he said, as the boy slumped limp in his grasp. He dropped the boy, and the huddled figure on the deck looked very much younger and smaller. "I reckon he's got his rights, he has," the old man said, in answer to Dorian's question. "I'm his paw, and I oughta know."

The waves became long rollers, and as the boat crested each one, Frank found himself staring at the close horizon with disbelief.

They were off the California coast, the old man had told them, and now they were returning to their docks.

The city towered high on the horizon, an endless bank of man-made mountains that walked on stiltlike piers out over the water and embraced the whole coast for all its visible length. A low bank of dirty clouds hung overhead. When they came in closer, he could see that the city had been built on massive piers, level over level, for some forty or fifty stories into the air. The façade that faced the sea was not unbroken. It had its own man-made coves, and here and there higher fingers gestured into the thick hazy sky. Perhaps a quarter of a mile north of the spot they were approaching, great dinosaur-like machines squatted in the surf, building yet another extension of the city outward.

"West Covina," the old man said. "That's where I'm taking ya's."

The boat rose and fell alarmingly as the city heights fell over them. A thick scum of garbage and refuse slid down the back of each wave, the boat blazing a momentary trail through it. On each side, fat pillars of concrete closed in, thick as small houses, bearing the watermarks of higher tides, and slimy-looking where recently exposed. They had slipped under the city.

The afternoon sunlight bounced off the water and reflected in crazy patterns against the underside of the roof—the floor of the first level overhead. It was dank smelling and sometimes worse, and darker the further under the boat went. Here and there metal stairs spiraled down around the supporting pillars, some pitted and corroded until they looked as if they'd collapse if anyone set foot upon them. The pillars broke up the waves, and now the boat rode through the growing gloom on gentle ground swells that lapped noisily all around them.

The old man had switched on a light mounted on the top of

the boat's small cabin. The purr of the boat's engines seemed to bounce back hollowly from every side. The thin boy was still unconscious on the deck. Dorian and Frank crouched near him, staring equally wide-eyed as the boat moved deeper under the city.

Two close-set eyes gleamed eerily in the boat's light. Then something splashed into the water and was gone. A moment later the boat nudged a floating body out of its way. It had once been covered with fur, but whatever it was, it was now too far gone to tell.

Crazy sounds echoed back to them, and sometimes they saw other lights dipping and gleaming beyond the forest of pillars. They were not alone. The old man guided his boat without hesitation on its winding course through the pillars, and Frank wondered how he could tell where he was going. His sense of direction was gone, now, and they were too far under the city for even a glimpse of a stray reflected beam of sunlight.

The boat drew up to a pillar that looked no different from many of the others. The concrete was pitted and eroded, and where the metal stairs were fastened to it, great rust stains streaked down the pillar's side.

"Blast that boy," the old man grunted. "He's shirking! He's awake, I know he is. Ahhh . . . You—" he pointed his finger over the cockpit at Frank, "you grab a line and make her fast!"

Frank looked wildly around. "A line? Where? And 'fast'? To what?"

"On the ruddy bow, ya goodfernothin'—!"

He found the braided synthetic rope coiled in a pocket at the very bow of the boat. He lifted the coil, and waited for the boat to ease in closer to the stair.

"Whatcha waitin' for? Jump, boy!"

The boat was angling in; its light did not directly fall on the openwork metal stairs. The stairs had no outside railing; only one against the wall of the pillar. The boat's bow rose, and then dropped; then rose again.

Frank jumped.

His feet skidded on the narrow metal slats of the stairs, one foot a step higher than the other. He grabbed with his hand, and his fingers closed on a flaking metal rail. Suddenly the rope in his other hand jerked taut.

"Pull 'er in, boy—pull 'er in!" the old man shouted. His voice boomed in hollow echoes.

It was easier than he'd expected. The boat—suddenly very much bigger to him—pulled in with a firm tug. A minute later the engines cut and the old man was leaping spryly onto the stairs to take the line. Frank had found nothing yet with which to fasten it.

The old man's hands were a blur as he fixed the line to the stairs a little higher up—"So's for high tide, y'see?"—and then he sprang back on the deck to lift the thin boy over his shoulders and bring him back onto the stairs.

Then they were climbing the stairs, Frank first and then Dorian, followed by the old man and his still unconscious son.

The slab-concrete ceiling was no more than twenty feet above the present surface of the water, but the climb on the steep and narrow spiraling stairs was a tiring one. Frank felt a lot better when he turned a corner of the pillar and saw a wooden trapdoor set close overhead.

"Jes' putcher shoulders to it, boy," the old man called from below. "It's not heavy."

The door must indeed have been counterbalanced. He shoved under it with one shoulder, and it moved easily up and out of the way. He climbed up into a dark room that smelled of fish. It smelled quite badly of fish, in fact.

Frank had once had an argument with an English teacher about the so-called five senses. The teacher was one of those men who seemed to disbelieve in science, preferring their own comfortably chauvinistic illusions about the world. He believed, for instance, that sounds did not exist unless human ears were there to hear them, and repeated that hoary old chestnut about the tree that falls in the woods where no one is near to hear. Frank argued with him on that occasion that the sound waves produced, the actual vibrations in the air, must have been there. The teacher had insisted that sound that did not reach ears were like radio broadcasts to which no radios were tuned. An ear, he said, was needed to convert soundless waves in the air into audible sounds. Frank, courting the sort of disciplining he often received for being too argumentative, insisted that a sound-wave vibration didn't need translations. Small sounds sometimes started avalanches in the Alps. Earthquakes made noises with the same vibrations that destroyed buildings. Sound waves could be mechanically measured, recorded, and reproduced. He knew he was right, but he knew of no way he could by argument alone convince his teacher. It was a common problem: The man had gained the status of *teacher*—therefore he knew that he must be right.

"We hear lots of sounds we don't even realize we hear," Frank had added. "Like bats, I mean. We use sounds to tell us things like the size or shape of a room."

And his teacher had laughed, and said, "Now you're talking about the sixth sense, aren't you? The sort blind people develop when they lose their sight?"

"It's just hearing," Frank had insisted. "They hear more because they train themselves to. They have to rely on it more. But bats make squeaks and then use them like radar to find obstacles in the dark, and people do it too, in a different way."

"Sure," the teacher had said laughing again. "Just last week I saw a blind man and he was squeaking down the street."

Everyone had laughed, and Frank had felt his ears burn. He wished he had the man with him now, in this dark, unseen room.

As soon as he'd set one foot on the floor of the room, his boot scuffing and making echoing scraping sounds, he'd known— he'd felt—the room was immense. The walls were far apart, the ceiling high overhead. Sixth sense? Nonsense! He'd heard all the myriad of echoes, bouncing and rebouncing, and somewhere deep in his subconscious his personal mental computer had noted the length of time in the cycle of echoes, from both sides and overhead, and if he didn't know the dimensions of the vast room in yards, feet, and inches, at least he had its *feel*. It was big, and there were no obstructions, no piled crates or the like, close by.

Dorian pressed close beside him, and then the old man grunted his way over the top step. "You follow me," he said.

Frank took Dorian's hand again and led her blindly after the other's footsteps. They walked across what must have been the broadest part of the room's floor, and then the old man stopped.

There was a metallic rasp, and a thin line of light appeared, growing until it outlined an opening door. The old man, still carrying the boy over his shoulders, stepped through and motioned them to follow him. Frank was only too happy to. The stench of fish was worse than that of any fish market he'd ever been near.

The door had opened upon a gloomy open corridor. In places

it was roofed over, but in others open shaftways extended upward past other floor levels, and stray light spilled down. It wasn't sunlight, but you could see by it.

The old man pushed the door shut and locked it. Frank looked around.

So this was the city of tomorrow!

He'd never been in one, but this corridor looked exactly as he'd always pictured a slum alleyway. Dorian shrank back against him.

Rubbish lay in heaps along the walls. Much of it had spilled from torn transparent plastic sacks. Among the rubbish lay men in tattered clothes. They were of an indiscriminate age. Frank had to step over the outstretched legs of one of them. At first the man looked dead. His eyes were closed, and his hair fell half over his face. He was lying fully sprawled, his head propped against an unsplit plastic bag of refuse. Only the slow rise and fall of his chest signaled the life still in the man. In his right hand he was clutching a small black box. A wire ran from the box up his arm and under his hair, above his ear. He was smiling.

"C'mon, c'mon," the old man said, turning to look back at them. "No time for sight-seeing."

Chapter Eight

"I WISH WE COULD GET to a visi," Dorian whispered. "If I could just get in *touch* with somebody . . ."

"You shush your mumbling," the old man shouted at her. Then he returned his attention to the limp figure of his son, sprawled out on the tiny aptroom's sole bed.

It wasn't a real bed; it was more like a heap of wadded cloth, spread out on the floor. And it wasn't much of an aptroom, either. The walls, like the floor and the ceiling, were bare cast concrete. A naked cable ran from a crude hole over the front door across the ceiling and terminated in a dangling glow-panel and a plug. Three wires hung from the plug to battered appliances. Food of sorts was cooking on one of the appliances now. It didn't improve the rank smell of the place.

There was something indescribably sordid about this place, Frank thought. It was too bare, too minimal, too mean a place to be real. He half expected the wall to fall back, revealing a camera crew eagerly grinding away. Like a James Farrell book: It was too gritty, too smelly; too, well, too *documentary*.

The boy hadn't revived. His father had slapped him several times before convincing himself the boy was still unconscious. Then he began worrying over the boy, shaking him, muttering at him, rubbing his arms and legs together, accomplishing nothing.

Frank wanted to feel sorry for him, but he couldn't. He felt sorrier for Dorian. She'd visibly withdrawn inside herself, shrinking from the unpleasant reality of the place.

"Boy, Boy, you gotta wake up, now. You gotta," the old man moaned aloud. "I din't mean to hitcha so hard, you know that. You was jest gettin' a little tetched again, and I hadda *do* it. I did! C'mon, now, Boy. *Please.*"

"I wish I didn't have to hear him," Dorian said. She pressed her face in her hands, and leaned tiredly against Frank. A little awkwardly, he put his arms around her and held her. She flinched at his touch, but didn't draw away; she seemed to need him now. She felt solid, under all her soiled finery. She was trembling, shaking a little.

"Dammit, now!" the old man shouted. "You gonna sleep, you might's well sleep happy!"

He unslung his pouch, and began poking in it. Shortly he removed a small black box. A wire was wrapped around it. He knelt again over his son, and fumbled with the wire. It looked almost exactly as if he was searching for a plug on the side of the boy's head. The wire stayed where he fixed it. He took the box and put it in the boy's left hand. He tried to wrap the boy's fingers around the box, but they were limp and lay open, flat.

Cursing to himself at this new setback, the old man closed his own hand around the boy's, the black box firm in their dual grasp.

The boy's eyes snapped wide open, his back arched in a violent spasm, and he shrieked. His scream was the most awful sound Frank had ever heard, and without thinking he tightened his arms protectively around Dorian.

When he looked back at the boy, he was lying as he had been, eyes closed, body limp.

But his chest lay still—he was no longer breathing.

The old man locked them in a second room. This room was even more featureless than the first. It was bare, its walls devoid of any feature but the door and an air duct near the ceiling. When the door closed, it was pitch black.

"Frank, what are we going to do?" Dorian's voice was small in the darkness.

"I don't know. What *can* we do?" He was exhausted; his mind refused to work for him.

58

"We've got to get away from this terrible place. We've got to get *home.*"

"Yeah," he agreed. "I'll buy that."

"If we could just get to a visi. We could call for help."

"Yeah."

They sat down, side by side, backs to the wall, on the dusty concrete floor. Somehow it seemed natural to them both that he continued to keep an arm around her. It was not cold, but the air was dankly humid, and it felt better when you snuggled close to someone else . . . especially when she was soft and warm, and felt good under and inside your arm. . . .

"Dorian?"

"Yes?"

"This is all as strange to you as it is to me, isn't it?"

"Yes," she said. "It's so awful. It's . . . hard to believe. You know?"

"It's been a full day," he agreed.

"They were really going to kill me," she said. "Transystems. Just because they made a mistake. I—I just don't understand."

"They didn't kill us, though," Frank said. He wanted to accent the *us,* but he didn't. "We're still alive."

"In this horrid rathole."

"Look, Dorian, let me tell you something, huh?"

"What?"

"It's been a big shock to you. I can understand that—until last night, whenever it was, nobody ever tied you up, nobody ever kidnapped you, nobody ever tried to kill you, nobody ever dumped you in the sea, and nobody ever put you in a hole like this. Okay, now dig this:

"Until a couple of days ago, nobody ever pushed *me* around like that either. Oh, I thought people did, but I didn't know how good I had it. You don't have even the vaguest idea. You see me coming from some sort of real backward time. like the cavemen or something. Let me tell you, I had my own room, in our own house, with lots of land around the house—trees, gardens, grass—and I had my own car, and where we lived was a nice quiet town without slums, without much crime or anything. I went to a school that wasn't overcrowded, and I was set to start college this fall, tuition paid and everything. I had a nice record collection, albums by the Harpers Bazaar, Van Dyke Parks, Charles Mingus, and like that, and a good stereo system. I—" his voice broke . . . "I had it pretty good, let me tell you. That was *my* home. And, and I'd give anything I've got to go back to it, just to be where I was before this whole thing started."

He felt tears swell, hot on his eyes, as he tried to keep talking: "Maybe we'll get you out of all this. Maybe we'll get you home, safe and sound. *Your* home is just halfway around the world from here.

"But I'm stuck here. I'm stuck in this lousy future, and as far as I'm concerned, *it stinks!* The whole rotten place stinks! And that goes for where you live, along with everywhere else. You sit up there in your ivory tower, and you think you're on top of the world." He choked out a weak laugh at the implied pun. "Well, I guess you are, at that. But your dear sweet daddy isn't any better from where I sit than Elton's is. Because either one of them, they both wanted me out of the way. They both didn't give a damn about me—I was just an inconvenient bug to be stepped on.

"Well, dammit, where I come from, that wouldn't have happened. And I don't *like* it, and . . . Oh, I dunno . . ." His voice trailed off into a choked sob as he exhausted his emotions. "It doesn't matter, anyway. It isn't going to change things any."

Dorian twisted around in his arm, and he thought she was pulling away from him. Then her groping hand found his cheek. Very gently, she wiped away the wetness that had rolled down the side of his face.

That was all it took. Suddenly, and without warning, he found himself shaking with uncontrollable sobs, while gentle arms held him against a soft warm body.

He tried to stop, and then he finally did stop. He felt deeply ashamed of himself, ashamed of his unmasculine, unadult tears. But they had been necessary. He'd carried the strain for too long, bottled within him. And, though he little knew it, even men must sometimes cry.

"I'm—sorry," he said at last. "I haven't, uhh, done that . . . well, for a long time."

"Don't be," Dorian said gently. "Don't be sorry. You couldn't help it. I know."

He reached up his hand to her face, touching her delicate features for the first time. His fingers found her eyebrow, and traced it out from the bridge of her nose and down in a question-mark curve on her cheek. Her cheek was wet, too.

They fell asleep, huddled against each other on the hard, cold, damp floor, and slept an uneasy, fitful sleep until the door rasped open. It might be next morning. It might be just two hours later.

The old man was standing in the doorway. He was braced across it, his hands on each side of the doorway. His head was lowered, like a bull about to charge. When he spoke, his voice was thick and heavy.

"Killed my son, ya dirty pargsfilth. Killed m'only begotten son." His voice fell into a whisper. "You know that? You hear that, huh?"

Frank climbed warily to his knees. Dorian shrank back against the wall. Tension filled the air like an electrical charge. Frank felt his skin tingle. "We didn't kill him. We never touched him."

"You killed him!"

"We didn't touch him," Frank repeated.

"I saw ya. You hit him. You plugged him in. You knew nobody turns on when he's out bad, you knew that!"

"No," Frank said, trying to project a calm voice he didn't feel. *The old man's as crazy as his son.*

"Yes!" the old man screamed, and he lunged into the room.

He dropped his head and his shoulders, like a football lineman rushing. He charged straight at Frank. It was too easy. Frank threw himself to one side and the man went right by him. He hit the wall with a thud, and fell down it to collapse at its foot like a thrown mudball.

"Oh, God," Frank said, staring down at the man.

"What did he do?" Dorian asked, her voice shaking.

"He didn't even see," Frank told her. "He didn't even see I wasn't in front of him. He just ran himself right into the wall." He felt his own heart pounding, his blood full of adrenalin, his legs wobbly.

"Is he—?"

Frank knelt and touched the man. "I, I can't tell. Maybe . . . Yes, I think I've found his pulse. It's kinda weak, but it's even. He's okay; he didn't kill himself."

"Oh," she said. And he wondered himself whether or not he was relieved.

It took both of them to drag him out into the other room. The boy's body was already bundled in brown cloth. It looked very much like the stuff they'd worn into the water, and it probably was. They laid the old man out on his bed.

"What about money?" Frank had asked. "Ought we to search for any?"

"Let's just get out of here—before he wakes up," Dorian said.

It seemed like a good idea, then.

How do you react to death or near-death? How can you? You're on the highway and a car perhaps a quarter of a mile ahead suddenly goes into a crazy spin, and you watch it with disbelief even as you're pumping your brakes. You stop a hundred yards past the smashed car and you rush back, your heart in your throat, scared and excited and relieved it wasn't you—*you* didn't get hurt—and then you see the arm hanging from the open door. The windshield on the passenger side is starred from the impact of a human head, and blood flows down the arm and drips from limp fingers. You stop. You don't want to get any closer. Suddenly, it's real. The blood glints in the sunshine the way it never did in the movies or on television. It makes dark stains on the gravel shoulder.

You're fascinated. It's morbid, but you can't help yourself. It's real, and you've never seen it before.

What if, when you saw the smashed face of the victim, you recognized it: *It's your best friend's mother!*

The human mind has layers of defenses, like an onion. When one wall is breached, another lies beyond. What was shocking and meaningful only an instant earlier becomes quite suddenly an abstraction, and you might be thinking, "What can I say to my friend about this?" and "I mustn't be offensively morbid in my reactions," and it's suddenly a matter of *behavior,* of proper social graces. This, too, may carry its own built-in shock, when you step back from your thoughts and look at them. But it is necessary. We must preoccupy ourselves with living, not with dying. Our minds are constructed for this purpose.

Frank Marshall had never before seen anyone die. He had never before had his own life deliberately threatened. He'd read both mystery novels and factual reports of crime and murder, and he'd swapped stories with his friends about "Now, what *I'd* have done—" But it was all just stories.

It had been a long day. Where did it begin—that day? The International Date Line had been crossed, and so much of the time they'd been locked away from daylight. Neither had a watch. Was it twenty-four hours after the kidnapping? More? Less? When you've gone through a lot, when you're a little bit shook up—or more than a little—you lose your sense of time. Hours become minutes, seconds grow into hours. It all happens too quickly—and too slowly.

A long day: kidnapping, the certain threat of death, even resignation to it: a near-drowning. And then these crazy people who could save your life one minute and be bargaining with you for it the next.

Think about it: Already the kid is distant in your mind, Frank. He was very real when he laughed at Dorian, and he was crazy real when he wanted your hand. The sound he made in his moment of agony was the worst sound you ever heard. But you don't talk about him. You don't think about him. You need your defenses. He was just the punctuation, he and his frightening father, to the worst day of your life—give or take a few hours. Now is not the time to think about what *you* would have done. Later, you'll wonder why, starving, you didn't eat some of that food, awful as it smelled. Later, you'll wonder what kind of idiots you were to walk out without a single cent of money, without even looking to see if there was some. Later, you can ask yourself, "So they saved our lives—how much did we owe them in return?" Right now you want to shut it out. There are two ways: Get away from the actual scene of it all, and don't think about it.

Chapter Nine

"I THINK WE OUGHT TO find the way up," Dorian said. "This level is awful. It doesn't even seem to have a public visi."

"Why don't we just try to find a cop," Frank countered.

"A 'cop'?"

"You know—a policeman."

She shook her head. "I don't think so. Not here."

"Why?"

"This is California. This is Transystems territory."

"You mean they control the police?"

"I told you, Frank. They're the second biggest corporation in the System! Who *else* would have police here?"

"Okay." He shrugged. "We'll try for a way up."

Broad stairs climbed a shaftway at the intersection of two public corridors. The next level was a little cleaner, and there were no bums lying about. There were no public visis, either.

Three levels further up, they found a public visi.

It looked a little like a public phone booth, except that it had a chair in it. Dorian sat down in the chair and Frank stood behind her. Facing them was a flat panel with a slot and a set of push buttons in two neat rows.

"Oh," said Dorian, in a disappointed-sounding voice.

"What's the matter?"

"I—I don't have a card."

"A card? What kind of a card?"

"I.D.—you have to put it in the slot, before you can make a call."

"Can't you get an operator, or something?" Frank asked.

"I'll—try."

She leaned forward and let her fingers skim down the first row of buttons without touching any. The last button of the last row was a bright red, in contrast to the others, which were gray. It was marked for emergency. She hesitated, then pushed it.

Immediately the metallic sheen of the bare panel above the buttons dissolved into a screen on which they saw an attractive young woman.

"Yes, may I help you? What is your emergency, please?" The woman stared woodenly out at them, her eyes fixed straight ahead.

"Uhh, it's not exactly an emergency . . . but . . ."

The picture of the woman flickered, as though tape-spliced. *"This is an emergency code. If you have no emergency, please disconnect."* Then the screen went blank.

Frank leaned over Dorian's shoulder, and punched at the red button again.

The same woman reappeared. She showed no signs of recognition. *"Yes, may I help you? What is your emergency, please?"* She stared woodenly out at them.

"Yes, we don't have the, ahh, card for the slot, and we want to make a call," Frank said, cutting off Dorian.

"This is an emergency code. Your request does not constitute an emergency. If you have no emergency, please disconnect."

Frank allowed himself the pleasure of several appropriate words in Anglo-Saxon English, then once more jabbed the red button.

"Yes," the same dead-faced woman said from the screen, *"may I help you? What is your emergency, please?"*

"Transystems tried to have us killed," Frank blurted. "We want to call Syncom for protection. Does that qualify as an emergency?"

The woman flickered, then was gone. A man in a blue uniform looked up. His eyes were intelligent, and they scanned quickly from Dorian up to Frank.

"Officer Gannon, Transystems Security," he said. "What's your problem?"

Frank leaned forward, his finger stabbing out for the disconnect button. In that split second, his eyes locked with Gannon's, and as the screen faded, Gannon was already turning quickly away from the picture.

"He recognized us," Dorian whispered.

"Don't be silly! How could he recognize us? He's never seen us before in his life," Frank said. But his voice shook with uncertainty.

"Something . . ."

"Can he trace us here?" Frank asked, cutting her off.

"I don't know!"

"We've done a very dumb thing," Frank said. He shoved open the booth door. "We just told Transystems we're still alive."

"How do you mean?"

"Up till now, we were officially drowned at sea—as far as the powers-that-be were concerned, anyway, I mean. Officially I suppose we're just 'kidnapped and missing.' But now—well, maybe that man didn't recognize us for who we are, but what do you want to bet he made a recording—or whatever it is they do with these things—and is checking it out right now? Somebody is going to recognize you, if not me. And that somebody is going to know we're alive, and at large, and making attempts to call home. Well, if they wanted us dead before . . ."

"Oh," she said. "I see."

"Well, I was right about the police," Dorian said, as they hurried away from the booth.

"Yeah, but wrong about the visi," Frank said.

"Hello," said a voice from just behind them.

Frank jumped.

"Are you children in some sort of difficulty?" She was a middle-aged woman whose black hair was even shorter than Dorian's. She was holding a plastic bag which seemed to contain small boxes and parcels. There was no immediate reason to trust her—her face was lined with mortality and looked no more honest than many he'd seen—but Frank felt very tired, and enormously weary of distrust and fear.

"Do you live near here?" he asked.

"Why, yes."

"Could you take us in, for a little while?"

Her eyes narrowed. "You *are* in some sort of trouble, aren't you? Runaways?" She didn't wait for an answer. "You come along with me, and you can tell me all about it when we're settled down and comfy."

Mrs. Kirru lived in a one-room apartment, an aptroom that measured the same dimensions as the main room of the old fisherman's place. There the resemblance stopped. While his had been a bare cubicle of concrete, filled with scavenged litter and little else, Mrs. Kirru's aptroom had plastic-coated cool lime-green walls, a spongy composition-tiled floor, and neatly built-in furniture. Indeed, it took several comfortable minutes before one noticed the absence of windows. The entire ceiling glowed evenly, and a wall hanging showed a lifelike picture of the ocean. Indeed, it was *very* lifelike, as Frank discovered when he glanced up at it to notice the waves moving. It was a closed-circuit receiver panel from the west coast panorama broadcast from up in Monterey. Many aptrooms had them; they helped make one feel less closed-in and claustrophobic.

Mrs. Kirru folded out two seats from the wall and beckoned them to sit, while she put away her packages. The walls of the aptroom were fitted with ingenious storage spaces; not one cubic inch went unused or wasted.

"Now then," she said, pulling out another seat for herself. "Tell me all about it."

Frank told her an edited story. They were the children of people high in Syncom, he said, and Transystems had kidnapped them in order to put pressure on their parents. They'd escaped and he told the story about their rescue from the ocean fairly straight. "You see, what we have to do now is to get back home," he finished. "Back to Syncom. But we can't even use the visi to contact our, uhh, parents."

Mrs. Kirru shook her head. "They identified you on the corner visi?"

"Yes," Dorian said in a low voice. She'd left most of the talking up to now to Frank, adding only a detail once in awhile to his story.

"Well, they'll be swarming there now. Oh my, I hope no one saw you come home with me. I haven't the tiniest nook for you to hide in, here." She shook her head again. "You children look a mess. I'm not surprised, after all you've told me. But we've got to get you cleaned up and into decent clothes. Otherwise they'll spot you immediately." She wore a conspiratorial smile. "We'll get you cleaned and fed, and then we'll think about how to get you back home again, eh?"

Dorian flashed him a quizzical look, and Frank relayed it to Mrs. Kirru. "Please don't think we're ungrateful or anything, but we can't help wondering—why are you doing all this for us? I mean, why should you *care?*"

The woman's shoulders slumped, and her face was suddenly old. "I should tell you, I guess. You have as much right to know as anyone. I'm a widow, you see. I lost my husband and my son—he'd be about your age, now—some years ago. It was one of those corporate espionage things . . . they didn't talk about it, but I knew.

"My husband was an engineer. He was very good; he was in molecular engineering. He worked for DelVaCo. That was back when they were trying to edge into Transystems' lunar territory. They sent him to the moon. We were all going to go; I'd never been to the moon, and of course Diki hadn't—he was just a little boy.

"Health Control slipped up. I caught a viral, and they quarantined me for a week while I was being treated. My husband went ahead. He took Diki. I was supposed to go up later and meet them. It was my idea that he take Diki. I didn't think the boy would want to stay here on Earth while his mother was in quarantine and he couldn't see her except through a screen.

"It was a Transystems ship, of course. And it blew up, midorbit. It had to be sabotage. Oh, they made lots of noises about how safe their ships were, and how somebody was trying to hurt them. They pointed their finger at Syncom, as I recall. . . . But the accident —that's what they called it, an 'accident'—wiped out the team DelVaCo was sending to the moon, and I guess that was a broad enough hint. DelVaCo had been getting a little too ambitious—that was when Draco Senior was running it—and I guess the thinking was, one of our ships is a fair trade for putting them in their place." Her voice was low and bitter.

"They were so *nice* about it, Transystems. They gave me the flight insurance. And DelVaCo gave me his pension. That was before Transystems bought out DelVaCo. No pension now. Just this tiny little aptroom, bought and paid for, free and clear, in a low-level neighborhood that gets worse every year. . . ."

"You think—Transystems destroyed their own ship?" Dorian asked, wide-eyed.

"It got them DelVaCo eventually, didn't it?" Mrs. Kirru replied. "What do *they* care about five hundred lives? They probably put their least-qualified crew on the ship. It was only luck—just pure, dumb luck—that I wasn't on that ship too. And many's the time I've wished I had been. . . ."

"It's so hard to believe," Dorian said.

"I don't think so," Frank told her.

Mrs. Kirru sighed. "Listen, child, you should know better by now. Why do you think everyone hates the Heirs? They don't care about us people. They're a breed apart—they think so, and I guess maybe they are. They're inhuman: monsters." She shook her head. "I guess you know that too. They play with us like we're toys. Break one, buy two more. I—oh, why do I go on? I let myself get worked up like this, I'm just being silly. It's like the air: You can talk about how awful it is all day long, but nobody ever does anything about it." She smiled. "It's just part of the world we have to live in, I guess. How about something to eat, huh?"

She fed them; then she manipulated a sliding door and revealed a closet-like cubicle. It was entirely tiled and looked rather oddly familiar. "Time for the 'fresher. You kids familiar already with each other?"

"Huh?" Frank asked.

"I mean, you share beds?"

Dorian turned beet red, and Frank felt his own face burn.

"I guess you don't. Hmmm. That complicates things a little; I hadn't counted on that. Goodness, you look old enough for a temporary contract. Well, son, suppose you just turn your back for a few moments while we pop your Dorian out of her things and into the 'fresher. I'll try to find a robe or something for you, dear. That's it. You need some help with those fittings? My, they're fancy. Isn't it a fact, they never make a thing for women that doesn't require a contortionist or a helper to get out of?"

While Frank faced away from the two, Mrs. Kirru kept up a

steady babble of conversation. He still felt embarrassed by the woman's assumptions. *Why, he hadn't put a hand on the girl.* Well, not really, anyway. She was more like a younger sister to him, a companion in disaster, sort of.

The door snicked open again, and a whiff of something that smelled like a blend of perfume and something medicinal came out into the small room. Frank waited until Mrs. Kirru said, "Okay, now. Your turn."

He turned around. Dorian was wearing a kimono-type garment that touched the floor. It hung on her like silk, although it almost certainly wasn't. She looked very slender, almost boyish, and strangely beautiful. Her cheeks were still glowing, and she wouldn't look directly up at him.

"Don't mind me, boy," Mrs. Kirru said. "I've seen boys before."

Nevertheless, freshly embarrassed, Frank quickly kicked off his boots and zipped out of his jumpsuit, darting into the 'fresher. He wondered if Dorian had been watching him.

There was one stud on the wall. He tried twisting it, then pushed it. Immediately the air of the tiny cubicle was filled with a dense mist. He felt no direct spray against his skin, but the mist seemed to penetrate every pore, even as it surrounded him. The smell was powerful, but not unpleasant. It didn't seem to hurt his breathing at all. Then the mist died away, and he found himself sweating profusely. Sweat poured from all over his body. He felt weak, feverish, his skin tingling, almost vibrating. Then the mist was back, but this time subtly different in smell and density. It coalesced on him in little beads and droplets, and began running down him in little rivulets. It made him feel exhilarated, excited, very healthy.

When the mist stopped again, jets of warm air began caressingly buffeting him, drying his skin a rosy pink. He felt cleaner than he'd felt in years—and "fresher" too.

When the door slid back, Dorian's back was turned and Mrs. Kirru was holding out a kimono that was the twin to the other one. Frank shrugged gratefully into it and tied the sash firmly at his waist.

"I'm going to go out, now," the woman told them. "I'll try to get you some nice, inconspicuous clothing. It won't be fancy or anything; I've already spent most of this month's allowance, but I'll find you something up on Level Twelve. They've got good bargain shops there." She smiled, and then winked at them, admonishing gently, "Remember, you be good; you've got no contract."

"I like her," Dorian said. "She's a little like Gam'ma—my governess."

"I wish she wouldn't talk like that, though," Frank said.

"You mean, about the . . ."

"Yeah. The contract, or whatever."

"I never knew it was allowed for anyone our age."

"It probably isn't, in your case," Frank said. "I gather it is something like, well, trial marriage, or something."

She blushed again. "I'd sooner not talk about it." She sighed. "Things are so different here. You know, I never ate food like *that* before."

"Neither did I," said Frank, misunderstanding. "Good, though."

"I mean, with a—what was it?—a spoon, by myself, I mean."

"That's right," Frank said. "I forgot. Around your place everybody feeds everybody else—with fingers."

"Heirs," Dorian said seriously, "never feed themselves. Heirs do not use tools or wait upon themselves. It is beneath them." She giggled. "Most of the time, anyway."

Frank felt the growing intimacy between them. It was almost like a sharp pang in his chest. She seemed so different, so close and so . . . well, desirable. It made him aware of her as a girl, in a way he hadn't felt before, even when they'd held each other and fallen asleep together. She seemed to feel it, too. Color kept coming to her face—it couldn't all be from the 'fresher—and he'd look up to find her eyes on him, then immediately sliding away in confusion.

He tried to imagine how he'd feel if it was Betti sitting so close to him, both of them wearing only these thin, almost sheer kimonos. Well, he could imagine their parents' reactions to such a situation easily enough. They'd scream bloody murder!

But he couldn't mock up Betti in his mind's eye, try as he would. He saw Dorian, pensive look on her face, staring at something about two feet to his left and halfway to the floor and probably nonexistent. Betti was far away and alien, as unreal as if she'd never been. So much for a six-month crush he'd thought he'd had. He felt like he was thirteen again and trying to put his arm around that little girl . . . what was her name again? Ann? He felt just as awkward and uneasy.

The uneasiness between them and their awkward awareness of each other grew until the tension between them was like a taut rubberband that threatened to snap at any moment.

Chapter Ten

"WELL, I CONFESS I JUST don't know what we should do next," Mrs. Kirru said. Frank and Dorian had been dressed in "good, middle-class garments," as she'd put it. Frank had donned a gold tunic and green tights, with his boots, and felt like Robin Hood in a grade-school play. Dorian was wearing an outfit which looked remarkably like his, but it was his firm conviction that it looked a lot better on her than it did on him. With her bobbed hair, the scarlet tunic, and pale yellow tights, she almost looked like what the women's maga-zines would have called Mod '69. His back had been turned, but her whispered protests of "Is this *all?* I can't wear just *this!*" as Mrs. Kirru helped her dress had done plenty to pique his curiosity, and he couldn't hold back a whistle when he was allowed to turn around. "Yeah!" he'd said.

But now it was time to share the seats again and try to map out their next step.

"You say you came from Syncom—that would be India Territory?"

Dorian nodded. "Yes. If we could get just to New Delhi . . ."

"Well, I'm sure I haven't money to book your transportation, even if it wasn't all Transystems flights anyway."

"They might realize we're still alive now," Frank said. "That visi-call was one of our dumber moves. Sooner or later they're going to try sealing off the area and searching it."

"I saw a number of men, loitering in the corridor, when I came back," Mrs. Kirru said. "They didn't look like drifters. They didn't have stim-boxes, for one thing. And I never saw a drifter who wasn't wired to one of those awful things. They're probably security men."

"Oh, great," Frank said. "That means we're penned up in here."

"Let's not worry about that for now," Mrs. Kirru said. "I think we can get you safely out of here . . . but the question is, where to? Transystems has all the flights, the hover-liners, the trans-Pacific freighters—everything that goes west from here."

"Then we'll go east," said Dorian.

"East?" Frank asked.

"Why not? They're less likely to be looking for us that way, and they don't control all the NorthAm continental traffic. At least, I don't think they do. Do they, Mrs. Kirru?"

"No, dear, they don't." Mrs. Kirru frowned to herself. "And I believe I'm starting to get an idea. . . ."

It *sounded* like a good idea, but as time crawled by, Frank began to wonder if indeed it was going to work. He didn't have his watch, and there was no way of knowing where Mrs. Kirru might have put a clock in her Chinese puzzle-box of an apartment, if indeed she had one. So he couldn't mark off the passage of time against a clock; he had only his not-entirely-dependable inner clock. It told him she and Dorian had been gone too long.

"I'll be back in an hour or two," she'd said, just before opening the door. Dorian had looked back at him for a moment, a little wistfully, he thought. Then they'd left.

"They're looking for two children—a boy and a girl," Mrs. Kirru had pointed out. "They won't pay any attention to a woman and her daughter, now, will they?"

And when she came back, she was to escort him out the same way. It had all the brilliance of an idea so dumb it had to work, he thought. The "Purloined Letter" trick—be so open and obvious about what it is you're hiding that no one notices it at all because they're looking for the furtive, the secret. Yeah; just maybe . . .

And then what? A transportation terminal, local, low-level,

short-haul, GLA owned—too insignificant for Transystems to own or monitor.

This was the first he'd been alone and by himself in quite awhile. He couldn't sit still. He stood and paced, the narrow walking spaces in the crowded aptroom confining him like a pacing lion in a cage.

Could they really trust this woman? What if she'd already turned Dorian in and was going to come back to turn him in? No, that would be stupid. She'd been out before; she could've brought the cops with her then.

It made him uneasy, the way he had to think about himself here. Like a criminal or something, on the run from the law. Well, no . . . maybe more like an agent in an enemy country. And they were out after him. Well, so far it was nothing like James Bond.

Where *was* she?

That Dorian, she sure was hard to figure out. She was so naïve about some things here, and yet she'd grown up in this lousy world. Still, she was a pretty good kid. She hadn't taken it all as badly as he could have expected. Under that candy-soft naïveté was a strong will and a wiry-tough mind. She was pretty cute, too, especially in that new outfit. She had curves he hadn't suspected. There was this movie, on the late-night reruns, one of those Robin-Hood-type movies, where the girl is some sort of a princess, and in order to go out to run away with the hero, she dresses up as a page boy. Somehow nobody notices until it's too late, despite the fact that in those clothes she still looked all-girl. Dorian reminded him of that scene; she didn't look like the girl in the movie, but the outfit wasn't so different, and she was definitely all-girl.

The door snicked open, and he jumped.

"I'm going to come in and sit for a moment," Mrs. Kirru said. "It wouldn't do to hustle right out again." She gave him a motherly nod and a smile.

"How did it—was everything okay?" Frank asked.

"Just fine, just fine. Nobody paid us the slightest attention. Your Dorian is parked safely out of the way, and just as soon as I've caught up my breath, we'll be on our way to join her. My, but this *has* been a day!"

He tried not to stare at the man lounging against the wall at the corridor intersection, but he felt the man's eyes burning holes in his back as he walked arm in arm with Mrs. Kirru around the corner. Mrs. Kirru was chatting away about all the neighborhood gossip, and when he tried to pay attention to what she was actually saying, he realized she was talking nonsense, babbling really, just letting the words flow freely. When a certain number of nouns, verbs, adverbs, and more nouns came out, she'd cut them short with punctuation and begin a new sequence. It sounded quite ordinary and natural unless you really listened. It was the one sign of the woman's nervousness, he realized.

This corridor was broader, and more heavily trafficked. He saw why when they came to the conveyor lift.

It was like an elevator, in slow motion. One platform after another crawled up past the open space in the wall. They were linked, one above another, in an endless chain. You waited until one was about equal with the floor, and you stepped on. Each platform could comfortably hold a dozen people. Several were already on the platform that drew even with the floor as Mrs. Kirru led him onto it. As he turned back to watch, the corridor floor dropped down, and a thick concrete bar slid down past his eyes to become a new corridor floor, the next floor up, and dropped inexorably past. A man brushed past him impatiently, and hopped down. Then yet another floor was coming down to meet them. It moved slowly, compared with an elevator, but the very fact that it never stopped made Frank glad enough that it rose no faster.

A woman stepped on, pushed past Frank, and stepped to the rear of the constantly rising platform. He turned to watch her, and received his second surprise: The back of the platform was as open as the front, and there, rising slowly up, past them, was another platform.

"That's the faster one; express. We don't want it; we're getting off at Level Fourteen," Mrs. Kirru told him. And all too quickly she was leading him off the conveyance.

They walked past a second niche in the wall in the next "block"; this one had platforms that descended. "Don't get close unless you're getting on or off," Mrs. Kirru told him. "Otherwise you just get in the way. They don't stop to wait, you know. Goodness, don't they have lifts in your part of the world, young man?"

"Not like these," he told her, and that was certainly the truth.

The GLA terminal was a large room of milling people, and

it reminded him of Union Station in Washington, D.C. People sat on benches, clutched bags or packages, and but for their dress might have been travelers from his own century. Mrs. Kirru led him around the outside of the room until she'd skirted half its circumference. Then she gasped.

"Oh, dear. Oh, my!"

"What is it?"

"Your young lady. She's gone! I left her here, right on this bench." She glared at a man who was slouched at its far end, the only occupant. A wire ran from his temple to a black box clutched in his hands. His expression was distant. *"He* wasn't here before. Oh, what could have happened to her?"

"Here I am, Mrs. Kirru!" Frank whirled to see Dorian quickly approaching them. "Hi, Frank—" she grabbed his hand warmly. "Oh, I'm so glad to see you . . . both of you."

"What happened?" Frank asked.

"Where *were* you, dear?" Mrs. Kirru asked. "You have no idea, the shock—!"

Dorian gestured at the sprawling man at the far end of the bench. "He sat down next to me. When I moved down, so did he. So finally I went looking for the, ummm, the woman's room." She colored a little, and later she told Frank she'd never been in such a room before—"They run you into open stalls like, like sheep!" Frank didn't bother arguing with her metaphor.

"You're all right?" Frank asked.

"I'm all right, now."

Frank nodded in the direction of the man on the bench. "What's he doing?" he asked Mrs. Kirru. "I mean, what's the box, the wire for?"

She frowned. "That's a stim-box. You have an operation— they're free—and they put a little stud in your head. Whenever you want, you plug in the box, and turn on. The box contains batteries, and when you grip it, it gives you a jolt of electricity. It goes into the part of your brain they call the 'pleasure center.' I'm told it makes you very happy. I wouldn't know, myself. It's not the sort of thing a decent person should become involved with. But—" she shrugged bitterly, "I see more of them around all the time."

"I guess it really beats drugs," Frank said.

Mrs. Kirru kissed them both on their foreheads. Frank had

to bend over a good bit. Then, her eyes warm and moist, she said, "Good-bye. You remember what I've told you. Mr. Archer will be watching for you. A big redwood of a man. And—good luck, children."

Then they stepped aboard the tube train and took their seats.

The train was surprisingly narrow; single seats ran down each side of the car with only a narrow aisle between them. Frank and Dorian found seats directly opposite each other, and Frank stared out his window at the platform and the people bustling along it. Across the platform was another train. Its cars were joined in short links to make a long, wormlike train. The sides were curved, the doors cutting into the low roofs, windows bulging out. The cars swayed a little as people got in and out; they were slung from an overhead truck that clamped itself between two narrow rail beams hung from the ceiling. If you looked closely, you could see through the gap under the suspended cars to the platform on the other side.

With a hiss, the doors of their train slid shut. With eerie smoothness, the train began accelerating out of the station. Before his car had passed the end of the platform, Frank guessed it was already moving at a speed close to or better than a hundred miles an hour.

As the train reached its cruising speed the acceleration decreased and the upholstered seatback stopped thrusting itself against him. The train could have been gliding on air, for all he could tell; there was no track vibration at all.

Immediately it passed the end of the platform, the train plunged into a black tunnel, and Frank knew no way to guess their actual speed. He turned and looked across the aisle and met Dorian's eyes. She gave him a brave smile, and he returned it.

Sounds were muffled, and except for the vague blur of the tunnel walls, lit only by light from the train windows, they might've been standing still in the station yet. He looked back at Dorian and saw that her eyes were closed. He wanted to doze himself, but he couldn't. It was like his first trip in an airplane. After the plane had reached cruising altitude, some six miles above ground, there was really little to see but clouds and the patchwork quilt that unreeled so slowly below. Frank's father had picked up a magazine and made a show of reading it, but Frank had kept his eyes glued to the window, the whole four-hour trip. For most of the time there had been nothing to watch, but somehow he couldn't look away. After all, there *might* be something in the next minute, and besides, it was all *new*. He had slept on the return trip.

It was new. That was reason enough to stare out the window at the rushing darkness, punctuated at rare intervals by glowing meteorites of colored light that swept by so quickly their afterimages were comet-tails. Signals: You could blink and miss one.

He felt strange, sitting in the soft, enwrapping seat. At last they were inconspicuously garbed—well, inconspicuously for *this* time and place—and moving anonymously among others. And at last they were on their way someplace. It was a little unsettling to realize that for the time being they were safe and yet on their own.

They were on the San Bernardino Express, and they would stop only once, Mrs. Kirru had told them, at Pasadena. He wondered if those places were much as they'd been in his time, or whether indeed they were even in the same places.

After a time, the train began slowing. It decelerated more gently than it had accelerated, and slid suddenly out of the tunnel and into a station in an easy glide.

Pasadena station looked no different from the train than the terminal had. After all, they were still on Level Fourteen; they'd never left the vast intercomplex of the megacity.

As the train picked up speed again, Frank felt his eyes slipping shut despite himself.

The sudden play of sunlight on his closed eyes brought him awake. He stared in surprise out the window and saw brown-tipped mountains close at hand. The train was out in the open, moving under a spider-tracery of overhead tracks, while steep slopes fell away below. The sun—how nice, to see the sun again—hung in the west, deep crimson and haloed by the thick bank of smog that swept to the horizon.

The train swerved, and then he saw the city, flowing like a concrete river through the valley below. They'd climbed above it, but individual buildings clung to the nearer hillsides in clusters like barnacles to a ship's hull. Even the crest of the nearest mountain was sheered flat and paved, small aircraft hovering around it like bees around a rosebush. Everywhere you looked, you saw the work of man. It was not an entirely pleasing sight.

When the train snapped back into a tunnel, it was like a slap of darkness, but the trip was almost over now, and soon the train was slowing once more. Frank regarded the end of the brief trip with mixed emotions.

It was impossible to miss Archer. He stood out on the platform like a giant among pygmies. He was a tower of a man, tall and thick-hewed, his unruly mop of hair a dirty blond thatch, his tunic soiled and threatening to split, his welcoming smile a beacon brighter than the sun.

"Ah, now; you're the kids I've been looking for, right enough!"

"You're Mr. Archer?"

"I am indeed. Soon's I talked with Mother Kirru, I hopped into the old crate and came up the mountain. And I'll bet it took you no longer to get here all the way from Ellay. Now then: You'll be Frank, and you're, ahh, give me a moment—I got a way of misplacing pretty girls' names—Dorian . . . am I right?" His face was bronzed by the sun, his eyes gray-blue, and his teeth white. His expressions were so animated that it took you some time to notice that the laugh lines remained engraved in his face even when he was sober, and that for all his talk of "Mother Kirru" he could not be so much younger than she.

"I want to hear your whole story," he told them with a deep laugh, "but first let's get ourselves moving, huh? Let's get outa all this traffic, an' catch our breaths." Effortlessly, he herded his two charges down the platforms and through the crowded waiting rooms, and out into the real outdoors, the crowds melting before them.

And finally Frank felt truly confident that their luck had turned.

Chapter Eleven

ARCHER'S "OLD CRATE" WAS A flat, saucer-like machine ten feet in diameter, with a transparent bubble atop it enclosing four seats. It sat flat upon the pavement of the GLA terminal roof, surrounded by parked buglike wheeled vehicles.

"I have to pony up a monthly allowance on the crate, just for having my own power source, but it's worth it," Archer said, as he gestured at it.

"Your own power source?" Frank asked. "They tax you for it?"

"Well, it doesn't amount to much more'n I would pay for public broadcast power," the big man said, waving his hand at the antennae on the wheeled cars, "but their story is, I'm adding to air pollution, so's I have to pay for it. C'mon, let's get in."

A quarter section of the bubble slid back, and Archer stood on the saucer's rim while he assisted Frank and Dorian into the two back seats. Then he shoehorned himself into one of the front seats, snapped the bubble shut with a twist of his wrist, and turned on the power. A low growl began, somewhere below the sonic threshold, a rumble that rose into a snarl, and then to a whine. "Gotta see to those turbines," Archer tossed back. Then the sound was a high-pitched but subdued hum, and the big man's fists curled over two knoblike controls. Frank glanced out through the transparent bubble and saw that the saucer rim was vibrating a little. Then, suddenly, stomach-wrenchingly, the rim *lifted*.

He'd expected it, Frank told himself, but still it startled him. Suddenly, without anything feeling at all different *within* the saucer, the world outside *tilted*.

"We're up on our air-cushion, now," Archer remarked, and as he thrust a knob forward, they began gliding smoothly out of their parking space.

The little cars, most of them no bigger than for two people, gave the saucer wide berth, Frank noticed. It dwarfed them, and its occupants towered over the huddled drivers of the three- and four-wheeled vehicles scuttling out of harm's way. Archer chuckled a little, and Frank wondered which it was that scared those other drivers more—the sight of the big saucer bearing down on them, or the giant of a man perched on it in full view like a king on his throne?

"We'll get out of this traffic in a bit, and be shut of ol' San Berdoo," Archer said. He twisted a knob, and the saucer angled itself around the twisting ramp and slid down toward the street below.

The thing was a ground-effect machine, Frank recognized. A hover-craft of advanced design. Somewhere underneath them were big fans, sucking air and blowing it down under them in a cushion that held them suspended a foot or two above the ground. The saucer was floating on its own blast of air. Smaller fans and vanes undoubtedly controlled its direction and speed. If it was anything like the experimental craft of his time, Frank knew, it could climb over uneven ground, glide over water, and mount low obstacles. It hardly even required a road—although here it was probably confined to roads by law.

Archer took them out of local traffic and up onto a high-speed expressway, where they picked up speed and the controls were locked into an automatic computerized traffic-control system. The expressway led east, through a gap in the mountains, and out into the former Mojave Desert.

It was hot, even in the air-conditioned bubble. The sun was angled low, but heat seemed to shimmer off every nearby surface. But a desert it was no more.

Plastic-roofed canals described geometric patterns on the ground below, and bounded precise checkerboards of varying hues of green. Buildings still dotted the landscape, and vehicles of varying types joined and left the stream on the expressway to shoot down exit ramps onto local roads that paralleled the canals.

They followed the expressway for at least an hour, Archer pointing out the various sights along the way, until at last the big man touched a control and the saucer slid sidewise into an exit lane, and then veered off down a ramp. Then Archer's hands were moving the controls again, and they were speeding up a nearly deserted local road.

A canal, plastic roof arching over it and dotted on its underside with condensed moisture, followed the road to their right. To their left, across the road, stretched a flat expanse of fields, row upon row of green plants converging on the horizon, irrigation ditches scoring the earth between every two rows of the crop. Several times they passed spider-like machines that stood on thin legs straddling the planted rows, mechanical arms lowered among them, toiling at some arcane task. If a man was inside any of the machines, he was not visible.

Then the terrain began to change. From time to time the fields of green would alternate with barren plots on which only gray-green clumps of desert brush grew, and the canal to their right had branched several times and grown smaller each time. Far ahead, close to the changing horizon, tables of land thrust up against the purpling sky.

The road turned and left the canal. There were no houses, no buildings to be seen at all, and no other traffic on the road. Dusk was falling, and Archer touched a switch and turned on powerful floodlamps that lit the road ahead. The road was older-looking here, and Frank almost could imagine they had spanned time back to his own century. The road was flat, uncrowned, and here and there sand drifted out across it, to whoosh up in sudden clouds as the saucer sped over and past.

"Gettin' there, now," Archer said, breaking the silence. Dorian's fingers clutched, and Frank realized he'd been holding her hand for some time, without quite being aware of it.

Then Archer slowed the saucer, and swung it down, off the road and across a shallow ditch. The hum was louder now, and Frank sensed they had risen a little higher because of the rough terrain ahead. They were following a desert trail, the way marked by the signs of earlier passage—the scoured look of the ground where the big fans of the saucer had blown away all the sand and dust and small rocks and pebbles—threading around and past thick stands of mesquite and creosote bush, clouds of dust billowing out behind them.

Ahead a flat-topped mesa loomed in the growing dusk, its top still bright with orange sunlight, its foot half hidden in shadows. "That's home, up ahead," Archer said, pointing. "Up on top— that's where I live."

"You live a long way out," Dorian said.

"Yup, I do. I like it that way," the big man said, nodding his head. "Likely enough people will get out this way another ten, twenty years, but for now it's got its privacy."

The trail followed halfway around to the right of the mesa, then began climbing where the slope was gentler. Whining and kicking up stones that clattered against its metal undersides, the saucer followed the winding trail until at last it crested the rim of the mesa.

Viewed from a distance, the table-top of the mesa had looked quite flat and none too large. But viewed close-up, the mesa top covered the area of several city blocks and was less than perfectly flat.

Tumbled boulders drew long sharp lines of shadow across the trail, and the saucer dipped down into a hollow and then climbed another rise before stopping before Archer's house—the sole sign of habitation on the desolated butte.

The house looked at first like an oversize igloo. It was a squat dome, dull white in color and glowing in the last daylight like a sunken harvest moon. A wall of piled stones marked off the boundaries of a weed-grown yard. Windows gleamed darkly from their dormer placements.

"Didn't have time to straighten up much," Archer said, his voice a growling apology. "Mother Kirru didn't give me a lot of time. . . ." He pulled open the door, reached inside for the lights, and ushered them in. Frank was just as glad; already a chill breeze had sprung up, and they weren't dressed for anything but the controlled temperatures of the megacity.

The house had the look of poured or molded plastic. The built-in furniture around the curved walls seemed joined to and a part of the walls themselves. "Standard FX-3 unit," Archer replied to the question. "Time was, it seemed pretty small. . . ."

The house had several rooms. An antenna atop the dome roof had fringe reception on the broadcast power— "But I don't think anybody knows about it; supposed to be you can't get it all the way out here." The interior dividing walls were straight, but the outer walls followed the curve of the dome; it was hard to get used to.

Archer seemed to be a sporadic housekeeper; piles of litter were arranged neatly, but at random on all handy horizontal surfaces; all but the table in the eating nook were also filmed with dust. "Sorry about the shape of things," Archer apologized again. "I got an electric housekeeper, ten years old, but you can't turn it loose with all the stuff stacked up, you know, so I tend to leave it put away and forget about it."

Mrs. Kirru had obviously briefed him; he showed them two separate sleeping rooms. Each was small but comfortably laid out, and each had its own 'fresher. The bedding was fresh, but both rooms had the air of rooms long unused, closed off.

"Mr. Archer?" Dorian asked when they returned to the living room. "Did you, uhh, did somebody else live here once? Too, I mean?"

The life left the big man's face, and he stared at her without speaking for so long that Frank grew alarmed.

"Yes, miss," Archer said at last. "Somebody else used to live here. Too."

"If I, well, if I shouldn't have asked," Dorian said, "I'm sorry."

"Nope." Archer shrugged and climbed to his feet, his hair brushing the curved ceiling. "No reason not to ask." He moved without haste into the eating nook and began opening and closing things.

Frank and Dorian exchanged looks. Frank stared past Dorian out a window. The night was black, and the glass mirrored the room dimly. Only the brightest stars were visible outside.

"You're hungry?" Archer called out.

They agreed in unison voice.

"Right. We'll have something for you in a minute. Real meat—how 'bout that?"

The meal was strained and mostly silent. The meat was stringy but not really tough. It was very light, like chicken, but gamier. It was in a stew of vegetables and rich gravy, and tasted better than anything else Frank had eaten in this era. Finally he worked up his nerve to speak over the oppressive silence.

"Ah, what kind of meat is this?"

"Lizard," was Archer's succinct reply. "Killed it myself, out on the mesa, 'bout five years ago. We had a good year for lizards that year. Froze quite a lot. 'Bout the only kinda meat I can supply these times."

Dorian looked none too happy at the news, but brightened a little when Archer added, "The stew was my idea; standard algae gravy, plus lizard and vegetables poached from one of the mechanized farms."

"I like it," Frank said. That made the big man smile.

"All right," Archer said, settling his bulk down in a soft foam chair. He let his breath out in a heavy sigh. "Let's clear the air a little. Let's talk. I'll go first."

He'd dimmed the lights and now only one low lamp etched out the highlights of his craggy face. "Ten years ago I thought I was a happy man. I was married, full-term, lifetime contract. I worked for DelVaCo; that's where I met Pop Kirru. I lived in the Greater Bakersfield Complex. I was always the family maverick, but I was doing all right, I was on my way up, Junior Managerial Engineering Level already and still rising. I put in for kids."

He saw the questioning look on Frank's face. "This is a crowded world, fella. You don't go about breeding it even more so. But I, we both had good genes, for all that I'm outsized and eat too much, and we got a permit from Health for a girl and a boy, spaced two years apart. Well, that was all right. I hadn't expected more.

"We had the girl first. We each had phys-checks, and Marie —my wife—had her ovulation timed and everything. Sex determination is controlled by conception, you know. Male sperm are faster'n female sperm, but they don't live half as long. It all depends on how you time it for the sperm to meet the ovum." He shrugged and screwed up his face into a scowl. "Very scientific. Nothing left to chance. I guess you're both old enough to know something about that, huh?

"Well, anyway, little Margo was born fine and healthy, and

we put in for another aptroom and got it—only one level down, anyway, and my career kept right on rising.

"About then was the big Lunar Shuttle Bang. You heard about that. It took out Pop Kirru and their kid. Mrs. Kirru stayed with us for awhile after that. She was pretty torn up about it. And then DelVaCo sold out to Transystems.

"Now, fact was I didn't *want* to work for Transystems. Too big, too many executives. It clogs the mill and stifles advancement. That's why I'd opted for DelVaCo, even though I'd heard stories about how it was going to get gobbled up. You always hear stories like that—mostly from the competition.

"So anyway, there I was, a tiny cog in a huge mess of wheels in Transystems. And came time for Timmy. We went through the whole hoopla, the same sex-determination bit, so's he'd be a sure-enough boy and not mess with the statistics.

"Naturally, I'd been transferred to Transystems Health Branch from the DelVaCo Health Branch, and Marie had her regular checkups at the new branch and all, and we never thought twice about it.

"Then Timmy was born."

He stopped, and stared into the shadows for a long moment. Neither Frank nor Dorian spoke. The silence hung in the room for a stifling eternity. And then shattered:

"He was a freak.

"Understand me, he was not rightly human. They'd given Marie shots, drugs that worked on the fetus. They'd said they were vitamins, stuff like that. He didn't have arms and hands. He had limbs of flexible cartilege and flippers. His head was long and pointed. He kept his gills—they're a stage every fetus goes through, but his didn't disappear. His legs were real short and ended in fins and flippers. Immediately after he was born, they put him in a tank of saltwater—God help me, it was straight ocean water!"

"*Why?*" Dorian asked, her voice breaking.

The big man laughed, humorlessly. "That's what I wanted to know. They told me Transystems was experimenting with breeding a new kind of human. They wanted men who could live in the sea. We've been harvesting the sea for centuries, but nobody ever tried this stunt before—not that I know of, anyway. 'Controlled retograde evolution' they called it. They'd had it all worked out, the necessary drugs and what they'd do to gene structure, I mean. The kid would grow up into a sort of humanoid fish! He'd be warm-blooded, have a fatty layer to protect him from heat loss, but he'd breathe like a fish. He was trapped—condemned to live in the water all his life.

"I was in a rage. I screamed at the doctors, and told them they were criminals—and they pulled out a set of documents I'd never seen before, and pointed out to me that my signature was on them, large as life.

"That's when I really went berserk, I guess. I smashed the tank. Marie was having hysterics, and at the time I didn't even know for sure why—whether it was me, or what they'd done to Timmy. But I smashed that tank, and I watched my baby flop around on the floor and strangle for a breath in the open air, and I knew it was the kindest thing I could do for him because he'd been bred to be a slave of the worst kind and it wasn't gonna happen to my son—not to an Archer!

"Well, they locked me up and told me I was due for a brain operation, and that was the absolute kicker. Marie killed herself, and little Margo was taken by the authorities, and I didn't get out until some friends of the family pulled strings and had me released, brain intact.

"This house—" he waved around him, "I bought it while we were in Bakersfield when Marie got pregnant. When they let me go, I quit Transystems—just ahead of getting fired, I'm sure—used my savings to buy this empty mesa top, and had the house lifted here. I like it, living here alone, as far from people as is convenient.

"So that's my story—that's me. How about you?"

Chapter Twelve

THEY TALKED FAR INTO THE night. They told him the same story they'd told Mrs. Kirru, and then they told him their still budding plans. The first item discarded was the possibility of a visi-call to Dorian's father. "Believe me, it would be monitored. Not because they know you're *here,* specifically, but because a call to Syncom— *any* call to Syncom out of western North Am—is going to be monitored. They've got to be."

But Archer approved the notion of traveling east. "That's why Mother Kirru steered you my way," he said. "Not just that I'm Step One on your trip, but I can help. I'm going with you."

For Frank, that simple declaration eased a load from his mind he hadn't quite realized he was carrying. A glance at Dorian told him of her relief as well. There was something about the giant that instantly inspired confidence. He was *competent.* He had about him the air of a man who could take care of himself.

"It's going to take money," Frank said.

Archer shrugged. "Money I've got. My father died three years ago and, in an unparalleled gesture that still has the family talking, he left his entire estate to me. After Death Taxes it isn't enormous, but it will take care of our expenses."

Then they discussed itinerary. Archer snapped on a microfilm projector, and showed them a succession of maps on the wall, tracing

89

routes with his fingers. "East is the best idea. Transystems is weakest in its transportation links eastward. We can use local transit lines on this continent, grab a hover-liner, maybe freight, to Europe Territory, and take pot luck from there. Once over the ocean, that's when we'll try the visi again."

Frank fell into an uneasy sleep, tossing and turning often on the pneumobed. Thin predawn light lit bands of sky in the east when he finally gave it up as a bad job and rose and dressed himself.

When he opened the door he saw the silhouetted figure of Archer hunched over a table. The big man turned and looked up.

"Ah, there, Frank. An early riser, I see."

"Have you been up all night?"

" 'Bout that, I guess. Is it getting light?" He leaned to peer out a window. "Hmmm, 'tis at that. Well, I haven't been wasting my time. Got things about worked out. Called my bank and withdrew a comfortable draft on my card. Made arrangements—few as were needed—to be away for awhile . . . mostly unpaid bills to be caught up. We're ready to leave any time now."

"You don't waste time, all right," Frank said. He yawned. "Aren't you tired, though?"

Archer shrugged. "Used to be, I got by on a couple hours sleep a night, and I could go forty-eight or more without sleep when I was hot on a project. Last few years, I've let it all slide . . . slept half the day away. I'm thinking this game of yours is good therapy for me. As I shouldn't be surprised Mother Kirru suspected. . . ." He chuckled. "I'll be good for the day, anyway."

"It's a pretty lousy world, though, isn't it?" Frank said bitterly. "I mean, when you come right down to it, I'm not going to get much out of this trip."

"It's got its lousy moments, I'll agree to that. But what do you mean, you won't get much out of the trip? I thought the whole idea was getting back to Poppa Syncom."

"For Dorian, it is," Frank said. And then he told the big man the truth about them. He told Archer he'd come from the past, and he told the solemn-featured man that Dorian was Damon of Syncom's daughter.

"As far as I'm concerned," he finished, "I'd be just as happy out here in the desert."

Archer shook his head. *"Time-travel,"* he whispered to himself. "Hard to believe. Huh! So why go back, then? You don't owe them anything, that's a fact."

"For Dorian, I guess," Frank said. "I don't know. Maybe—if I got her back safely, I mean—maybe her father would be a little happier about me, and my being with her . . . maybe. . . ."

"Yeah, I can see that," Archer said reflectively. "You have a thing for the girl, don't you?"

"I don't know . . . I guess so."

Archer nodded. "And she won't be happy except back at home. Well, you know, that's the first time I ever laid eyes on an Heir—to know it, anyway. And I don't suppose I'd have guessed." He grinned. "No pointy horns, no long tail . . . that I could see, anyway. . . ."

"You people really hate the Heirs, don't you?"

"I don't give a lot of time or thought to it, but I reckon it's true enough. Don't you? Dorian excepted, I mean?"

Frank nodded. "I guess I do. They don't really give people much choice, do they?"

Archer shook his head. "An old saying: 'Power corrupts, and absolute power corrupts absolutely.' They're the living proof. They set themselves up as minor gods over the rest of us. Born to it, bred to it, I guess by now it's part of their genes. But that's the way the world is. Most of the time you can't fight it; you just have to learn to live with it. Like the air, you may not like the smell, but you go right on breathing it."

Archer took them in the saucer across the desert to Vegas Complex, where they put the craft in storage parking and took a moving beltway to the downtown airstrip terminal.

The airstrip was another form of transportation new to Frank. Long flat-bottomed, tubelike ships, shaped like wingless airplanes of the size of a DC-10, sat waiting on flat metal strips while passengers were loaded and unloaded.

Archer explained the principles of the airstrip: "They use a form of magnetic repulsion to get it up at the beginning, just to get it off the surface of the strip. Then, once it's moving, it builds up a shock wave of air and rides on that. Like my saucer, only its forward motion throws the cushion of air under it. The things do about five

91

hundred miles an hour, about an inch above the surface of the strip. Very smooth, very fast, very efficient. Cheaper than the air, and, from our point of view it's better, since it's more localized and less controlled or likely to be watched, if you know what I mean." He bought their passage with his I.D. card, and the three of them took three seats abreast, together on the outside of the left aisle of the resting torpedo.

When they began moving, engines thundering in the rear, it was slowly at first, and then with increasing speed. You couldn't avoid the sensation of speed, because the ship moved right along the ground, on its own perfectly flat surfaced strip, zipping past buildings, the desert landscape, and all the scenery so close at hand. It was a thrilling and not a little scary way to travel.

The line turned southward, avoiding the higher mountains, skirting to the south. The land changed many times during the trip, the very desert itself shifting from clay and sand to naked shelves of rock, the vegetation from sparse silver clumps to low forests of scrub to tall sentinel cacti. And everywhere, the hand of man. Only water was a limiting factor. And science had learned to extract water from the dry silicate sands and clays themselves. Desalinated water was also pumped hundreds of miles inland from the oceans and the Gulfs of California and Mexico.

Although the airstrip avoided the higher mountain ranges, mountains were often in view. And when they sailed down into that hellish bowl of land that makes Phoenix a furnace and its citizens all a little touched by the heat, it was to enter an area thick with the haze of civilization.

The doors were opened for departing passengers and those climbing newly aboard. Archer gestured Frank and Dorian to keep their seats—they had through passage, but no reservations on the seats. To leave them now would be to lose them. With the new passengers came a withering wave of dry hot air. Outside the windows Frank saw the land shimmer with the heat. *That* hadn't changed in five hundred years, anyway.

Then they were on their way again, on the next leg of the trip, stops scheduled at roughly hourly intervals thereafter. Archer leaned back and dozed, but Frank held Dorian's hand and peered past her out the window at the speeding scenery.

To while the miles away, Frank asked Archer questions. Dorian said little. Sometimes she seemed to be dozing; other times she simply stared out the windows at the swiftly moving landscape. Frank wondered why she was being so distant, but could think of no way to ask her; the few attempts he made to draw her into conversation she answered monosyllabically.

"Air pollution?" Archer said, in answer to one of Frank's many questions—the man was a human encyclopedia in Frank's estimation— "We've always had it. I guess since man's had fire, we've had air pollution. The funny thing is that, knowing all we know, we *still* have it. You'd think anybody who'd dream up ways to go to the other planets could think his way around air pollution."

"In my time," Frank said, speaking in a low voice so that other passengers wouldn't overhear him, "we were already trying to do something about it. They were talking about banning cars from California in five years—nonelectric cars, I mean."

"Well, they've pretty well done that," Archer said. "Broadcast power was started in the first century after space travel—by Consolidated Electric, if I remember my history rightly; they were merged with Transystems in 206 A.S.—and nobody burns fossil fuels anymore. Why, you can't even *find* natural petroleum deposits anymore."

"There's no more oil?" Frank asked, a little incredulous.

"Oh, sure, we've got oil. Oil comes from plants—and animals. We grow plants for oil. We just bypass nature's processing, that's all. All the oil we took from the ground—it started out as plant life. But we don't have it to throw away, and we sure don't burn it."

"What about your hover-craft?" Frank asked. "You said something about not using broadcast power."

"I don't. It's not dependable when you get as far out as I live. I use a heat-conversion turbine; a thermal unit system."

"What's that?"

"Well, you know that it's always getting warmer or cooler, right? The temperature, I mean. There's always a differential. Maybe it's colder outside; maybe it's warmer. Out in the desert the extremes are pretty wide; it gets cold at night."

"Yeah, I noticed that," Frank said.

"Right. Well, when you enter a warmer environment or a

cooler one there's a heat exchange from warmer objects to cooler objects. Right? There's energy expended. That's the principle on which a thermal unit works."

"Yeah?" Frank asked skeptically. "That sounds a lot like the old gag about the perpetual-motion machine: Something for nothing."

"Nonsense; it's just taking advantage of entropy. Everything —even a hunk of straight iron, say—is losing a little energy all the time. Call it 'leakage,' call it 'waste'—when you convert matter to energy or vice-versa, you never get a 100 percent transfer; something's always lost. Right? Entropy. The universe is running down slowly.

"Only it isn't. That 'lost' energy isn't really lost; it's just gotten free of your closed system. Look at *you:* You're a furnace, and you're throwing off great amounts of excess heat.

"How do you think this airstrip is powered? They're air-conditioning us, aren't they? There's maybe three hundred people in here and we're all throwing off heat. Without air-conditioning, that heat would parboil us in an hour or two. Not that we wouldn't suffocate first, of course. But what do you think they *do* with that heat? The air-conditioner traps the heat—takes it out of the air—and *then* what does it do with it? I'll tell you: It sends it through a thermal unit about one hundred times the size of the one in my hover-craft, and turns it into energy."

"Electricity?"

"Some of it. Some is used as heat. Heat's energy too, you know."

"So how come you still have air pollution?" Frank asked.

Archer's eyes twinkled. "Thought you'd never ask."

"You got us off the subject."

"*I* did? You're the one who's asking all the questions, fella."

"Air pollution?"

"Okay." Archer laughed. "Air pollution: Sure, we still have it. Lots of reasons for that. One is that we're using the Sierras now for a pine ranch. Pine's a fast-growing source of cellulose, you know, along with petroleums, the base of plastics. Pine trees pollute the air."

"You're kidding."

"Nope. They 'sweat.' All trees sweat, you know. That's how

94

a tree keeps cool in hot weather; just as we do. They just happen to sweat turpenes and esters, resinous vapors which, in sunlight, cause a haze.

"Then too, there's all the people we having living on the face of this planet now. Each, in his own private way, does something—even if it's only just breathing in and out—that fouls the air and helps pollute it. Every few years they isolate another factor in the operation of one thing or another that's polluting the air. Last I heard, it was the algae farms. A by-product of the chemical conversion process by which the algae feed on sewage. So they do what they can to control it. But each little thing . . . you add them up, they make for a lot. Let's face it: There's over forty billion people living on the face of this planet. We're cluttering up the whole landscape!" He gestured out the window, and Frank saw the blurred dots of buildings scattered across the southwestern desert. "We try to stack our population in megacities, so the whole country won't be filled up, but, well, I expect even where I live will be all city and twenty levels deep within another twenty, thirty years."

"Where will you go then?"

"I dunno," Archer said. "I try not to think about it."

Frank stared past Dorian and out the window for awhile then, trying to assimilate all that Archer had told him, trying to build a more concrete picture of the world in his mind. Finally he spoke again:

"What about you? I mean, you don't have a job, and . . ."

Archer shrugged. "I won't starve. It would be a disgrace to my family."

"Isn't there a government welfare plan or something?" Frank wondered aloud. "Not for you, I mean," he added hastily.

"A 'government welfare plan'?" Archer echoed. "Did they have that sort of thing back in your day?"

"Sort of."

"Did it work?"

"I don't know. I know my father didn't think so. 'Pretty soon more people won't be working than will be,' was what he'd say. He said supporting his own family was enough."

"They taxed the workers to support the nonworkers?" Archer asked.

"I guess so."

"No wonder it didn't work. Where's the incentive? But that's foolish; it's been centuries since man was required to provide real labor. Modern management supplies about the only 'work' available these days, anyway," Archer mused.

"Well, what do people do for money now?" Frank asked.

"Depends on your class. If you're bottom level, I guess you pick up the leavings from above. You don't starve: Food can always be found somewhere—if you're not too particular about what it *used* to be. But I wouldn't know; I've never asked. In the so-called middle class, you work. You get a job with one of the bigger or smaller corporations. Or you start a small business of your own. That's more or less what I had in mind. There's still room for it. This is a free capitalistic society, you know. As long as you don't start crowding somebody bigger—somebody who can put his foot down on you —you can do pretty much what you want."

"I thought the big corporations had everything sewed up," Frank said, a little surprised.

"Well, they *do*. If you want to do anything big, that is. But say you want to start a clothes shop, and you're clever with an electroform and have an eye for fads in fashions. You raise the money and open up your shop, and you're in business. If you're really good, you'll do all right. And if you started nudging a big chain, like Sears & Hall, they'd probably hire you, to get you out of the competition.

"Keep in mind, it takes all kinds of businesses to make the world run, from the biggest to the smallest. The little stuff, well, big corporations just can't be bothered with it. Like that tube you took out of San Berdoo. GLA owns it. Now why would Transystems let GLA run that tube, you might ask, right in their own backyard?

"Well, Transystems runs flights to the moon, and to the colonized planets, and most of the planetary HST-suborbital rockets too. But a dinky tube train less than a hundred miles long? They *built* that line, did you know that? Sure: when they scalped Greater Ellay and rebuilt it into its present form. But they found out they were wasting their time and their money trying to operate every local piece of transit in the area. First they leased them out to private operators—like Great Los Angeles Co.—and eventually they sold the properties to them. It was a lot simpler."

They left the airstrip ship at the Cleveland Sector terminal in Erie Complex, the megacity that stretched around the southern and western edges of that dead sea. Like the southern California complex, it was built in layers that stretched out over the water and land like a concrete tide. But because the megacity's foundations were set in older cities, there was more variety and less uniformity from level to level and area to area within the megacity.

The terminal was on the First Level, buried under the mountain of the city. They took an express lift to Level Forty-eight, the upper-transit level, and there an individual tube-taxi to the Superlative Hostelry, a middle-class hotel, where Archer had reserved a suite of two rooms—two large closets in Frank's opinion—the most he could manage.

They had food brought to the rooms and then, exhausted, fell into their beds. Frank and Archer had fold-down wall beds in the front room; Dorian had a permanent bed in the second room and the room all to herself. "At least I'll be able to take a deep breath without bumping into you two," was her only comment on this luxury.

Again, Frank slept poorly. After an indeterminable amount of time had passed, he sat up, pulled on his tunic, and thought. Finally he got to his feet and went to the door of Dorian's room.

Should he knock? He didn't want to wake Archer. But he didn't want to walk in totally uninvited, either. His breath seemed to be coming too quickly, and after a time he wondered how long he'd been standing there at the door, his arm raised like a statue's.

He tapped, lightly.

"Frank?" It was just more than a whisper.

He eased the door open. "Yeah. Can I come in?"

The night-light glow showed him her nod. She was in the bed, covers up around her neck. He slipped in through the door and shut it behind him.

"I . . . couldn't sleep," he said.

"Me neither."

He sat down on the edge of the bed. She moved over a little to make room. She reached out one arm from under the covers but didn't touch him. "It's like I was never alive, before," she whispered.

97

"I feel so strange. The world—it's all so different than I thought, and every time I close my eyes and try to sleep, my stomach does a flip-flop and I see pictures of things rushing at me and past me, like out the window of that airstrip ship. It makes me dizzy, and I get the chills. Then, when I pull the covers all over me, I'm too hot again. Everything's crazy."

"The excitement," Frank said. "It's catching up with us. Reaction, I guess. What do you think of Mr. Archer?" he asked, changing the subject.

"I like him. He's so big and . . . well, protective."

"Yeah, I know what you mean. I—told him about me. This morning, before you got up. About my being a time-traveler, I mean. And, well, it just came out with the rest of it: I told him who you really were."

"You did?" Her voice trembled. "And he—didn't start to hate me?"

Frank shook his head. "He's not that sort."

"You're right. I'm glad you told him. It's better to be honest with him. Really and truly honest, I mean."

"That's why I told him. He's put himself way out on a limb for us, just because he likes us. I figured he deserved the truth."

"Yes," Dorian agreed.

There was a long pause. Frank tried to think of something to say. He was acutely aware of the fact that he was alone in a darkened bedroom, with the girl. He'd wanted this, and yet he was uncertain of what it was he should do next.

"Frank," Dorian whispered, breaking the awkward silence, "I'm . . . glad . . . you came in. Your being here . . . it makes me feel better. I don't feel so funny in my stomach or anything. Is that crazy?"

"No," he whispered back. Her short-cropped hair was black against the whiteness of the sheets that framed her, her face a pale blur. Her eyes seemed to be locked on his, but the light was so very dim. He leaned forward, his body tense, until he could see her face clearly, and the heat of her breath brushed against the skin of his own face.

"I—I wanted to tell you," she whispered, the words tumbling out now. "I wasn't mad at you or anything—today, I mean, while you and Mr. Archer were talking. But I had to be by myself and think. You know what I mean? I—it's all so new to me. It's as new to me as it is to you. The way these people *live!* And . . . and . . . the way they hate—us." Her voice broke.

"Yeah," he said, not knowing what to say to her. He wanted to touch her, to reach out his hand to her, to caress her cheek— maybe even to kiss her. But something held him in check. She wasn't a girl who'd ever been kissed—and he remembered how she'd flinched at first when he'd touched her before. She was a new kind of girl, and he felt an awkward thirteen all over again . . .

She reached out her hand, then, and touched his. She squeezed his hand. "Thanks," she said. "For coming in." It was a dismissal. And, the tension in his mind somehow gone, he rose and slipped out of her room and back to his own bed.

This time he slept well.

Chapter Thirteen

AT CLEVELAND THEY BOARDED A hover-freighter to England. "I thought about making it to the East Coast, but why bother?" Archer said. "I found this transoceanic freighter that carries a dozen passengers, and it was as easy to book passage here. They leave this afternoon."

The hover-freighter was a ground-effect machine, like Archer's saucer. The difference was that the freighter was a quarter-mile long, and weighed thousands of tons. Powered by a fusion-power turbine system, its fans could lift it only eight inches above a flat surface, and it was restricted to its docking facilities and water.

The stench of the Dead Erie Sea was overpowering when they left the taxi-tubes at the docking area. They were standing on a broad apron of concrete that lay only inches above the water surface of the lake. "It's on lifts," Archer said, "always right near water level." All around them were giant cranes and the shriek of hover-fans. "They never turn off their fans," Archer pointed out; "they can't really support their own weight any other way." He had to shout.

Giant containers the size of boxcars were stacked in piles, stories high, the cranes poised over them, loading and unloading the containers aboard the giant freighters.

Archer had to stop a man to ask the way to the freighter Morrison. Then they followed a twisting path through freight-loading areas, dodging zipping trucks and leaning cranes. There were few men about; many of the machines appeared fully automated and capable of working without human overseers.

The Morrison was a giant gray-painted hulk that sat on its roaring fans and received container after container into its capacious belly. An open elevator on a wheeled metal scaffolding shoved up against the freighter's side took them up and on board. There a man in a techman's jumpsuit showed them to a large single room.

"One room was all I could get; we'll just have to be one big happy family, I guess," Archer told them. Both Frank and Dorian found themselves blushing, but neither said anything.

Something new had crept into his relationship with Dorian. He'd known it since she'd stepped out of her room that morning. He had felt a sudden heightened awareness of her, a special sort of knowledge of her presence in the room. His skin had tingled; then he'd turned to see her. Her eyes had met his, and she'd blushed. A moment later he felt the heat in his own face.

Why? It seemed so silly. All he'd done, was to talk to her maybe ten minutes. They'd touched hands; nothing more. Why was he feeling like this? Why this sudden, overwhelming feeling of intimacy between them?

Well, if Archer had noticed the way he'd stumbled and stammered or Dorian's sudden coloring at his stolen glances, the man had been too polite to remark upon it. Thank God!

The freighter departed that evening, an hour before dusk, moving smoothly down off the docking apron over the water, and northeast up the long lake. The trip into Lake Ontario, and from Ontario up the rebuilt St. Lawrence Seaway into the Gulf of St. Lawrence, all took place during the night while they slept, and when they arose early the next morning, Newfoundland was already a tiny dot on the western horizon. The freighter would take a due-east course now for the Megapolis of England.

The passenger section of the freighter was in the forward end. There was no outside deck, but an inner deck with large windows surrounded the staterooms and at the bow it widened to become a glass-walled lounge.

"Your kids, mister?" a man with shoulder-length hair asked Archer.

"I'm their, ahh, uncle," Archer replied. Frank and Dorian were standing, side by side, at the forward windows, staring out at the sea.

"Wondered," the other said. He leaned forward. "Good market for kids that age, know what I mean?"

Archer stared down at the man. "No, I don't. What is it you mean?"

The man coughed. "Nothing illegal, friend. I represent one of the larger corporations, you know; I do a little scouting for them. Always on the lookout for talent, right?"

"What sort of talent?"

"Heh, young talent. You ken; clean young stuff for the Heirs. Nothing wrong about that, is there? Get to live with the top crust, huh?"

"You scout for the Heirs, do you?"

"Let me tell you, friend, my connections go right to the top. And the price is right, too. Set you up for the rest of your life."

"I don't suppose you'd have an excuse for me to give to their parents?" Archer asked, his voice carefully neutral.

"I can handle the whole thing, you know what I mean? Fake an accident, something like that; no sweat on it. And we put your money in a new account so nobody's suspicious about your earnings."

Casually, almost as if scratching himself, Archer lifted his hand and swung it backhanded into the other's face. The man let out a squawk and fell back over his heels against a bulkhead, his hair flying.

The commotion attracted attention. Frank and Dorian had turned and were staring. A ship's officer in a gold tunic was hurrying up.

"Sirs! Gentlemen! What *is* this?"

The smaller man picked himself up. "No harm done, no harm done, friends. Just a minor disagreement, am I right?" He forced a weak chuckle. "My card, sir," he said, thrusting a small pasteboard at Archer. "Should you have a change of mind, eh?"

Archer glanced at the card, and his face whitened. With the thumb and forefinger of each hand, he ripped the card in two, and told the man, "Get out of my sight and stay out of my sight. Take your meals in your room and stay there. If I see you again on this ship I'll pitch you overboard. You understand?"

"Gentlemen, *please,*" the ship's officer said.

They both ignored him. "Haste makes waste," the long-haired man said, smiling his reptilian smile again. But he moved quickly out of the lounge.

The officer shrugged, and turned away.

"What was that all about, Mr. Archer?" Dorian asked.

"Just a little unpleasantness," Archer replied. "Nothing to worry about." He was still holding the two halves of the card. He glanced back down at them. The half that was uppermost said "-rold, *special representative,* Syncom Corp." Scowling, he crumpled both halves and shoved them into his pouch.

Wouldn't that be cute, he thought, *to sell the Old Man back his own daughter for a concubine?*

There wasn't a lot to do aboard the freighter. You could stand in the lounge, staring out at the sea for awhile, marveling at the way the weight of the freighter and the air-cushion on which it rode smoothed out the waves close by. But the sea makes a dull companion when you're standing over a hundred feet above it and behind glass.

Then there was the "funny box" in the stateroom, and Frank had tried it just once, because he thought it might be like television and he'd seen nothing of the popular entertainment of this world.

He watched it for ten minutes, and the second five were spent only on admiring the device's technical qualities. Basically, it used the hologram concept, something they'd begun pioneering in the late 1960's. You trained two lasers on an object and took its picture. When you beamed a laser through the picture, a three-dimensional phantom appeared beyond it. You could walk around it, peer over and under it, and even move *into* it. Stranger yet, the hologram principle was based on the fact that *all* the information was contained in *every part* of the hologram film. He'd bought one from Edmonds Scientific, one which you held in front of a bright, reasonably tight beam of light, and stared through, like a slide. It was a chessboard with chess pieces sitting on it. He'd carefully cut the film in two. Each one showed him the same chessboard, the same chess pieces, only just a little smaller. His piece of film had been cut from a much larger piece, each piece containing all the information the larger film held. It was an unsettling notion, something of a real scientific breakthrough.

It stood to reason that if you had all the information on a single bit of that film, rather than spread out all over it, you could invent a new way of broadcasting television, and get 3-D with it as a bonus. The standard television set worked by scanning a picture that had been broken down into a grid of horizontal lines, picking up the information from each line with a horizontal scan, and then broadcasting this serial information to a set which built the picture back up again, line by line, scanning each line with a path of electrons which made the phosphors of the picture tube glow for an instant. Basically it was a cumbersome process of breaking a picture down into all its component bits of information, and then reassembling it again, painstakingly. Color television was the same thing, multiplied by three, since three separate beams of electrons had to be focused on the picture tube to make the red, green, and blue phosphors glow in a reasonable facsimile of lifelike color.

But suppose that instead of going through the whole scanning process like that, you could take a single bit of information from anywhere in a picture, and it would give you the whole picture? With really genuine color? In three dimensions?

Frank stared in open admiration at the way the funny box materialized a miniature stage in the air before the box, and set solid-looking objects and actors to moving upon it.

But in terms of content, ten minutes was all he was good for, and five had been plenty. The program—and Archer said it was true of every program—seemed deliberately aimed at morons.

Frank was staring at the funny box, wondering whether he should turn it on again, just for the novelty of it, when someone tapped his fingernails at the stateroom door.

He looked up. Archer and Dorian were forward in the lounge, but if either one had returned, surely he or she would not bother to knock. He went over to the door and thumbed it open.

"Hello, there, young man," said the man at the door. "I'm Victor Jerrold. May I come in? I'd like to talk to you."

It was the long-haired little man who'd been bothering Archer. Frank wondered what he wanted, but wasn't sure he needed to find out. "Sorry," he said, and started to thumb the door closed.

"Ah, ah!" Jerrold said. His hand clenched around Frank's wrist; his foot was wedged to hold the automatic door open. The door gave up the struggle and retreated once more into the jamb. "Let us not be rude, my young man," he admonished Frank. He stepped inside and the door closed behind him.

"Look here," Frank said, feeling his temper already rising. "What's the idea—breaking in like that?" He rubbed his wrist where the little man had held it; the man had a firm grip.

"Settle down, young fella; settle down," Jerrold said. Suiting his actions to his words, he let himself sprawl on one of the beds, and gestured Frank to sit down opposite him. "No need to kick up a fuss, is there?"

"I didn't ask you in," Frank said, unwillingly sitting as he'd been told.

"No, you didn't. And I suppose that's because of the, ahh, difference of opinion your uncle and I had." His beady eyes seemed to bore into Frank. "I wonder: Did he tell you about my offer?"

"No," Frank said. What was this unpleasant little man getting around to, anyway? "What offer?"

"Ah!" Jerrold said, as if he'd explained it all. "I see. Would you like to hear about my offer, then?"

"If you'll just say your piece and go?" Frank asked wearily. What *was* the man up to?

"My card," Jerrold said, handing a duplicate of the one he'd given Archer across to Frank.

Frank scanned the print. Then he looked up, not sure if he understood properly. "You're with Syncom?"

Suddenly the man looked wary. "That's right," he said, and then waited.

"Did Dorian's father send you?" Frank asked. That had to be the answer, he thought. The Old Man must be cutting up the globe in bite-size pieces in his search for his daughter. He wondered why they hadn't been contacted earlier. But . . . *if Jerrold had spoken to Archer, why hadn't Archer said anything about this?* He trusted Archer; Archer was helping them, wasn't he? Doubt kicked at the bottom of his stomach. He liked Archer; he'd trusted Archer. *Archer wasn't playing a different sort of game, was he? Could Archer be using them, for his own purposes?* He didn't want to think it, but the thoughts were there, and he felt sick.

"Young fellow," Jerrold said. He'd risen; his hand was on Frank's shoulder in a comradely gesture. "You can trust me. You know that now?"

He didn't want to. He didn't want to listen to the man. "Don't touch me," he said in a dead voice.

Jerrold paled, and his expression tightened, but he stepped back and sat down again. "Tell me about it," he said.

"I guess you know everything that counts," Frank said. "Except maybe who did it. It was Transystems. They kidnapped us." A flicker of emotion in Jerrold's face. "All we want now," Frank continued, "is to get back to Syncom and Dorian's father."

"I see. It shouldn't be too difficult," Jerrold said. "I, ah, I couldn't be sure, you see. I asked your, umm, your 'uncle,' but I guess he was naturally reluctant to speak of you. I gave him my card, but he was still uncooperative. I can't imagine why, if he's simply trying to help you return to India."

Not Archer, Frank thought, twisting his hands together, unconsciously working them, popping his knuckles. *Not him. We trusted him.* The irony of it: This weaselly little man had come to deliver them from big, bluff Archer. It wasn't right.

"What will you do now?" Frank asked.

"There isn't much I can do. Not until we dock, anyway," Jerrold said. "Then I'll take over and we'll put you on a direct transport for New Delhi and that'll be the end of it." He spoke crisply. "As for now, well . . . I suggest you say nothing of this to your 'uncle.' Take, ah, the girl into your confidence if you can, without arousing that man's suspicions."

"You're saying Mr. Archer is definitely . . . ?"

"Definitely not to be told for now; that's correct. I cannot satisfy myself that he has your best interests at heart. If he does, well, then no harm will be done, and he'll agree to things himself. If not . . . well, no harm there, either, eh?" He winked. Then he let himself out.

Frank stared at the door for a long time after it closed behind the man.

Chapter Fourteen

FRANK SAID NOTHING ABOUT JERROLD'S visit to Dorian or Archer. Archer was suddenly a man he could not trust. And he had no opportunity to speak to Dorian separately. The long-haired man's revelations should have made him feel better: Once they were docked in England, the trip would be all but over. But he felt miserable. He *liked* Archer. It wasn't just that he'd trusted the man, it was more than that. He'd admired Archer.

It was hard to forget that when he was in the big man's company. He would keep silent, the terrible fact of Archer's apparent betrayal churning in his stomach, and then Archer would say something, somehow drawing him once again into the conversation, and when he saw the twinkle in Archer's eyes it was easy to pretend he'd never spoken with Victor Jerrold; Archer, by his very presence, invited his confidence.

So he would pretend. He wasn't sure to whom he was pretending, but mostly, he decided later, he was trying to pretend to himself: pretending Victor Jerrold did not exist, and had indeed never spoken to him. Jerrold helped: the man stayed out of sight. Frank had only to pretend that things stood with Archer as they'd always stood—and to try, desperately, not to question to himself Archer's easy compliance with their cross-country flight and his apparently bottomless resources of money and knowledge.

So he sat with Dorian and Archer in the lounge and joined their conversation:

"Where will we dock?" Frank asked. "London?"

Archer gave him a puzzled stare and then a laugh. "I keep forgetting you come from long ago. London? There's a slum section by that name, but it's in Eastern City. No, we'll be coming in to the Bristol Sector."

It was easy to forget: *Five hundred years had passed.*

As Archer had told them, a suborbital flight could have taken them from Ellay to New Delhi in an hour . . . *taking either direction, west or east!* An atmospheric flight would have taken only a couple of hours. Instead, they had taken what would have amounted to a series of bus and subway trips between cities in Frank's time: local transit, slower, less convenient, more commonly used by local commuters within a single continental area. It was the "slow" way— although still fast by Frank's standards—but it had thus far—or so Archer said—kept them free of surveillance. All reservations had been made in Archer's name, and there had been no way for Transystems to get a lead on Frank or Dorian.

It was the parallels that threw him off, Frank realized, seizing upon the subject to divert his troubled thoughts. This freighter: It glided on air, it was shaped like a monstrous sausage, its blunt rounded front end was glassed in on the passenger deck, and they never had a chance to feel the blast of fresh air ripping past at somewhere over two hundred miles an hour. But it *felt* like a ship, like a passenger-carrying seagoing freighter of the twentieth century.

Then there was that incredible "airstrip" vehicle. An "airstrip" was more properly a landing field for airplanes, in Frank's mind, and he asked Archer why they'd taken an airplane and stripped off its wings like this in order to scoot it along the ground. "In my day, we had planes that went faster," he pointed out.

"Sure, and in your day, if I'm not mistaken, they were already having in-flight traffic problems, too, weren't they?" Archer replied. "And terrible crashes? The concept of a vehicle or string of vehicles that moves along its own right-of-way and can be completely controlled and scheduled is just a whole lot more viable. With an airplane, you have to have a big landing field, out away from population centers—and that's getting pretty near impossible anywhere in the world, now—and you have to spend a lot more time and fuel, proportionately, in takeoffs and landings than you do in cruising from here to there. It just isn't worth it for short-haul, like within a thousand miles or two. Instead, you set up an airstrip right-of-way, like an old railroad right-of-way, and you send airships down it, zip, zip, zip, directly from one in-city terminus to another. They're just as fast, and far more controllable and convenient. Stop and think about it."

The language crossed him up, too. These people didn't speak English; they spoke Universal, a common language originally invented, Archer said, by language experts and a large computer. The undertaking had been backed by Transystems, in one of its early moves to compete with Syncom. "When you have a company that spans the globe—not to mention the nearby planetary colonies— it makes sense for all employees to speak a common language," Archer told them. It was a story quite as fresh to Dorian's ears as to Frank's. "Lines of communication are important. And if you want your people talking it well and not as an ill-learned second language —this was before they had proper learning machines, remember— you teach it to them as young as possible."

Syncom had tried setting up its own corporate language, but was shortstopped by the fact that Transystems' language was about the best the experts could come up with, and also by the move by the United Nations—then still a force in world politics—to adopt the Transystems language as Universal.

It had been a long while now since Frank had spoken in English. Indeed, he had almost stopped *thinking* in English. For the instant transfusion of Universal through Damon's learning machine had given him the language as a first language—it was as thoroughly ingrained in his mind as English had ever been. And when you must converse solely in another language, it is easy to fall into thinking in it as well. The human mind is adaptable.

The word in Universal for "Cleveland" is not "Cleveland"; it is instead "Cyrvalendt," and it is pronounced *Shrive-el-lint*. But when Frank heard that name, it became instantly, and without his conscious thought, "Cleveland."

And because there *was* still a "Cleveland," and approximately where it had once been, as well as so many other names of places he still "recognized," the very differences, the changes wrought by five centuries upon the places, tended to seem less real, less important. He found a touch of the familiar, and overlooked the reality of the alien. And this too is a function—a defensive function—of the human mind.

But—*a slum section called London?*

Things were not as they once had been, in the Megapolis of England.

"As I understand it, somewhere between three and four hundred years ago, these islands were a separate nation—during the time of nations, anyway," Archer said. Fog and drizzle blanketed the window with moisture, but Frank tried to peer through it at the distant bulking arms of land that were guiding them into the Bristol Channel. His heart hammered. They'd be docking all too soon now.

"Back in those days the nation of England was apparently about bankrupt among nations, and desperate to keep itself and its people alive. Cut off from the Continent as it was—and still is, pretty much—and not being able to support itself without massive infusions of imports, it was in a pretty sorry state.

"This was during the rise of the corporations and the U.N.-impelled breakdown of national boundaries, but there were still a lot of trade restrictions across national boundaries."

"I don't understand," Dorian said. "What were these 'national boundaries' you're talking about?"

"Well, when you come right down to it, they were nothing more than arbitrary lines, drawn centuries earlier, fought over periodically, and kept there to create a sense of identity for those people they enclosed.

"The human animal seems to have these ideas about privacy and territory. They've been trying to wipe it out for a long time, but I don't expect they ever will. A man wants to own the spot where he lives; he wants to know it's his and he's safe in it. He wants to feel it's his private place. There's an old saying, might even have been around in your time, Frank: 'A man's home is his castle.' Meaning, it's his fortress, or, maybe, his cave.

"Get a bunch of people together, and they'll draw a big line around the area, enclosing all their many holdings, and they'll say, 'This is ours; this is *our* place.' And they'll name it, call it a town or a village or a city or a sector. And it's their common home; they'll fight to defend it from outsiders. You take a place's name away from it, or try to, and they'll fight you just as hard as if you actually took the *place* away. Symbolic, I guess. Like, when the old-time cities grew and overlapped each other, they tried to name the megacities new names that would include both or all the old cities. But the people who lived in what had been each separate old city, they wouldn't let the names go. It didn't work. That's why you have all these named sectors within a megacity, instead of neat alphabetical designations, and that's why the sectors aren't geometrically laid out. The people who lived there just plain fought it. And, something of a surprise, they *won*."

(Frank remembered his father telling him about Manhattan's Sixth Avenue in New York City. "They changed the name before the war to 'Avenue of the Americas,' and that's what all the street signs say, and all the letterheads of firms that have offices on that street say, but every man, woman, and child in New York City calls that street 'Sixth Avenue,' and if you want to find it, well, that's what you better ask for. Why, even the city subway maps call it 'Sixth Avenue,' " his father had observed. It was the same sort of thing, exactly.)

"Well," Archer continued, " 'states' and 'nations'—pretty much the same thing, really, just different words—they were just bigger chunks of land that somebody, probably a king, drew a big line around and declared to be a specific nation, or 'country,' as they called it. Sometimes somebody else—another king, maybe—considered the area, or part of it, to be inside the line *he'd* drawn, or maybe the people living on the contested spot didn't care for one king as much as another—well, anyway, they'd start fighting about it, the idea being to get it changed. I guess they had a lot of wars over just such silly ideas as where that line should be drawn, and just what an area ought to be called."

"There was more to it than that," Frank protested. "A lot of people didn't want to get that line drawn around them because the people who were doing it were pretty bad types. Like, my father fought in World War II, which started because one country decided to conquer all the others in Europe. The people of that country— Germany was the country—they'd round up people from all over Europe and put them in concentration camps or kill them. Our country, the United States—in North America—got into that war even though the Germans hadn't gotten across the Atlantic yet or

111

anything, just because we thought what they were doing in Europe was pretty terrible." Well, that was an oversimplification, but how could you explain it to people who'd never been there, and for whom it was all more than a little senseless, when you hadn't even been born at the time yourself? They showed television specials about it, and you saw the captured films of emaciated people dead on barbed-wire fences, and the gas chambers, and it made your stomach turn and made you want to see Germany smashed all over again, even though the Germans of your generation had seen no more of such things than you had—they hadn't been born yet either. And your father, who'd been there, who'd been part of the D-Day assault and lived through it, told you about Dresden, which the Allies had annihilated with a fire storm—a way of killing cities at least as horrible as the atom bomb—and smoked reflectively on his pipe and said, "When you come right down to it, Frank, the real horror of that war was that the Germans, no matter what you hear, they were no different than us. There's nothing they did that others haven't done—that we haven't done ourselves in our past—the only difference is that they did it bigger, gaudier, and in a way you can't brush under the carpet and forget after twenty years. But we're all capable of it, Frank. There's absolutely nothing more noble about us. It's an accident of history that Hitler happened to Germany instead of somewhere else. That's something to remember when they show films like that."

How could you explain such things to Dorian, to Archer— each of whom had been born into this, an infinitely more repressive and totalitarian world?

Maybe it was like Archer had said: You had to make do; you had to find a way to live, in any time or place. That which you were born to, you accepted. Well, to each his own. For all its faults, Frank preferred the twentieth century. He wished he could draw a line around *that,* call it "home," and step back inside.

"What's the matter, Frank?" Archer asked.

Frank stood up, half blinded by the sudden tears in his eyes. "Nothing," he said, forcing his voice to remain even. "I—I'm just going to lie down for a little while." Suddenly he wanted to be alone. The terrible lie of Archer's friendliness had overcome his defenses and he needed to be alone so that he could face the truth again.

"We'll be docking in no more than half an hour," Archer said.

"Yeah, I know."

"Frank?" Dorian said softly. "Is anything wrong?"

He wanted to tell her, but he couldn't. "No," he said. "It's nothing important. I'll tell you later." Then he found his way out of the lounge and into the connecting corridor.

He wasn't looking where he was going, and when he bumped into someone the apology was half out before he looked up to see it was the little man with the long hair: Victor Jerrold.

"I—I'm sorry," he said. "I wasn't looking."

Jerrold laid a friendly hand on his arm. "No harm done. I was, ah, just setting things up for us, on shore." He gestured at the door opposite. The plate on the door said "Communications."

Frank stared at the door for a minute, but said nothing.

"Where are your companions?" Jerrold asked.

"Up in the lounge. I just left them."

"Oh?"

"I was headed back to our room."

"I'll join you," Jerrold said, falling in beside him.

The unpleasant company of the man did nothing to improve Frank's spirits, since he was a living reminder of the problem Frank faced. But he did not brush Jerrold off; something was nagging at the back of his mind.

He put the sudden question to Jerrold when they were seated again facing each other on the two beds in the stateroom: "Isn't the communications system on this freighter Transystems?"

"Sure," Jerrold said easily.

The idea he'd been playing with grew in proportions: no longer a gnat buzzing tinnily, it was now bumblebee-sized. "Weren't you being a little hasty?" he asked.

"Hasty?"

"Contacting Syncom via Transystems communications lines?"

"Syncom? I wasn't—" Jerrold broke off suddenly.

Frank stared at the man. Neither spoke.

Then Jerrold grinned. "Blew it, did I?" His hand didn't seem to move, but something compact and blunt-nosed appeared in his right fist. It was aimed at Frank.

"What's that?" Frank asked. He felt frozen.

"Eh? Oh, a sonic."

"What's 'a sonic'?"

The man frowned. "What kind of a question is that?"

113

"What would it do to me?" Frank asked.

"Just knock you out, maybe give you a bad headache when you woke up," Jerrold said. He laughed. It was a nasty sort of laugh. "You just sit there, right where you are, and you'll never have to know."

"I guess I was pretty dumb," Frank said. He felt empty inside; the doubt had consumed him, and now he was empty and it had been all for nothing. Archer hadn't betrayed them: *He* had.

"I guess you were," Jerrold agreed. With his left hand, the man brushed his long hair back in an impatient gesture. "You're not with Syncom."

"No, I'm not with Syncom," Jerrold nodded.

"Who *are* you with?"

The man laughed again. "I'm with Victor Jerrold," he said, and laughed some more.

"I guess that's pretty funny, all right," Frank said bitterly.

"You're right; it is," Jerrold said. "It amuses *me.*"

"Well, now what're you going to do?' Frank asked.

"Just about as I'd planned to do," Jerrold said. "I'd expected to separate you and young Miss Dorian from your guardian. I'll just wait till they come for you, zap the big guy, and then we'll be off. Just the three of us. Cozy, eh?"

Frank shrugged. "What's in it for you?" he asked.

"Well, that hasn't been negotiated yet," Jerrold said, tossing his hair back again. "But I'm sure my reward will be handsome."

"Yeah? Your reward from who?"

"Let's don't play coy, my young friend," the smirking man said. "I have no intention of turning you over to the minions of My Lord Damon. Ah, no. I'd heard the rumor Transystems was hot for a pair of runaways; your Mr. Archer put my back up, but I had no idea you two were the ones till you all but blabbed it to me. What fine fortune it was that I happened to give you a *Syncom* card!"

"You've got more?" Frank asked. It was a rhetorical question, but Jerrold fished with his left hand in his pouch and soon held up a fistful of the cards. He flung them at Frank. Frank picked up one as it fluttered into his lap.

Victor Jerrold, it said. *Special Representative: TRANSYS-TEMS.*

"I've got one for every major corporation—at least one!" Jerrold said proudly.

"So you played me for a sucker," Frank said, the English words coming unbidden and strange to his tongue.

"Huh?" Jerrold said, suddenly alert.

"You fooled me," Frank said, translating.

Jerrold shot him a hard and questioning look, but nodded. "I did. You were easy for a man of my talents."

"You were talking to Transystems?" Frank asked. "Before I ran into you?"

"It's not easy to gain both access and privacy to a ship's communications equipment," Jerrold said, grumbling. "But I checked you two out; that I did."

"I presume you've got all your plans made for turning us over to them?" Frank inquired.

"I'll take care of that; never you worry."

"Huh!" Frank snorted. "You don't trust *them* either."

Jerrold tensed. "Mine is a delicate business, young man. The first rule is, 'Never give away your advantages.' They want you; I have you. Very well. We shall bargain. And when I am happy, they shall have you."

The sound of the door opening drew Frank's involuntary glance—and time stood still for a single moment of decision.

Archer—and Dorian. They're here. In a minute he'll shoot Archer. Then it will be too late.

Jerrold's head had turned to follow Frank's look at the opening door. His right hand was concealed by his body from those at the door. There could be no warning. Frank threw himself forward at the man, shouting a wordless shout as he did.

Frank had never gone out for sports; he'd always considered himself too slow, too uncoordinated. But he was young and he was strong and he wasn't small. With no idea of what he was doing, he threw his full weight on Jerrold, shouting his warning to Archer as he bore the smaller man down, and knocked him flat on the bed, weapon imprisoned under his body.

Something very, very cold seemed to freeze his left side, but his forward momentum had toppled the smaller man under him, and with his hands he groped for the man.

He was bursting with the violence of his emotions, and his hands sought out their target without his conscious direction. All the pent-up misery, helplessness, fear, and sense of betrayal focused on the tightening grip of his hands. He was not aware of anything

115

else in the room; his ears roared and his side was numb with pain, but they were not a part of him. His hands were a part of him: He was focused down through the converging channels of his arms, his thick wrists, into his tendon-tight hands, with which he took his revenge upon the whole world.

"Frank! Stop!"

Hands pried at his hands, and a voice screamed in his ears. The hands were bigger than his hands, and, as he recognized both them and the thin, fearful voice, he let them pull him loose from his rag-doll victim, and then he went limp.

Chapter Fifteen

"YOU WERE CHOKING HIM, FRANK. You were choking him and shaking him back and forth and I was sure you'd killed him," Dorian said. She was crying, and the tears welled up in her eyes to spill softly down her cheeks.

"I wanted to," Frank said. He was stretched out on the bed. Dorian sat next to him, looking down at him. Archer sat on the bed beyond, next to the unconscious Jerrold, whose breath came in slow terrible wheezing rasps.

"But, why?"

"It's hard to explain. Oh," he groaned. "My side hurts."

"Your side?" Archer said sharply. "Does it feel cold and hot at the same time?"

"Yeah," Frank grunted.

"I was afraid of that. He got you with the sonic."

"What—what will it do?"

"Nothing permanent. Lots of pain right now. It messes up your nervous system."

"Oh." He thought to himself. "How long—till we dock?"

"We've docked," Archer said.

"That's why we came to see what was keeping you," Dorian explained. "We thought maybe you'd fallen asleep."

"No such luck," Frank said.

"Care to tell us about it?" Archer said. "What was this vermin up to?"

He didn't want to tell them. He didn't want to tell Archer the dark suspicions he'd harbored. "If we're docked, shouldn't we be getting off?" he asked instead.

"No problem. They'll be unloading for three or four hours. We've got at least that long," Archer said. "Plenty of chance for you to get back to normal."

So he told them. In short, simple sentences, he told them what a fool he'd been and how much trouble he'd gotten them into. And what he'd had to do at the end.

"A bit violent, weren't you?" Archer suggested.

"I understand," Dorian said, leaning over Frank and looking down at him. A final tear fell on his face. "It wasn't just that man— it was all of them: my father, the man who kidnapped us, the man who dumped us into the ocean, that crazy man and his son who fished us out and were going to hold us for ransom. . . . You were striking back at all of them, weren't you?"

She was perfectly right.

"You were telling us about England," Dorian said.

"Oh, yes," Archer said, nodding. They had time to kill while the sonic weapon's effects wore off Frank. Archer picked up the threads of the discussion as though they'd never been broken—and Frank was grateful to him for saying nothing more about Jerrold and the way he'd believed the man.

"Well, as I was saying, England was cut off from Europe, but dependent upon trade with Europe and the rest of the world for survival. Just for food, for instance—they couldn't grow enough to feed themselves, and this was back before Fluxmeld began its worldwide food distribution system. So, since there *were* restrictions on trade between each separate nation, England decided to beat the game by declaring itself a 'free port.' What this meant was, 'Do your trading through us, and there won't be any restrictions.'

"Well, this set up a tradition and although the gradual disappearance of national boundaries made a 'free port' less important, and corporate territories were becoming more important anyway, England managed to hang on by becoming an Open Territory as it is today. This is one area where, although a number of major and minor

118

corporations supply the goods and services, no single corporation dominates. The Chamber of Commerce, a locally elected governing board, regulates corporate traffic and supplies the security forces, the police.

"The result is that the place is teeming with corporate spies of every variety, but it's the first safe place to contact Syncom. 'Neutral ground,' you might call it."

"Are we safe here, then?" Frank asked.

"How do you mean?"

"Jerrold." Frank gestured at the limp figure of the little man. "He told them—Transystems, I mean—he had us. Won't they trace his call and figure out where he is, where we are?"

Archer chuckled. "No. Fortunately, since the ship was already in the Bristol Channel when he made the call, it wouldn't have gone out as a ship-to-shore call, but would've been handled by the local communications exchange. And since I doubt he'd have tipped his hand to them about the ship he was on, well, that leaves a lot of ground—and water—to be covered. We're as safe here as anywhere."

"What will we do with him?" Dorian asked.

"I think we'd best just leave him here," Archer said.

"Is that a good idea?" Frank asked.

"No," was Archer's reply, "but can you think of a better one? We can't smuggle him off the ship—we haven't even any luggage. Best thing to do is to roll him under the bed and trust to his not being found for some hours yet. Maybe not even till tomorrow."

At that very moment, Victor Jerrold emitted a loud groan.

It was not repeated. After a long silence, Frank asked, "What did you do to him?"

When Archer answered him, his reply was grim. "I gave him a dose of his own medicine . . . a sonic blast."

Frank pushed himself up on his elbows. "You didn't kill him!"

"No. He's still breathing, but he'll have a wicked headache when he wakes up."

Bristol Sector broke the pattern, Frank decided. It was not extended upon piers over the water, and it was not built in layers upon layers. Instead, it looked rather like a twentieth-century city, although its buildings were crammed closer, and reached higher, rather like trees competing for sunlight in a dense forest. Well, he'd take part of that back: There *were* layers, because the auto-taxi, a computer-controlled automatic wheeled vehicle, did almost immediately speed up a ramp from the dockside to a sequence of decked roadways. But the roadways were open to the elements, and in fact it made him nervous that there were no windshield wipers on the blindly controlled little car, and the front windows were almost frosted with rain. He liked to see where he was going.

Archer, on the other hand, seemed more interested in where they'd been. He was twisted around facing backward over his seat, and staring intently out the moisture-beaded back window.

"What's wrong?" Dorian asked.

"Nothing. But I wanted to make sure we weren't followed."

"Are we?" Frank asked. "Could someone? Follow us, I mean —wouldn't he have to punch in a destination like we did?"

Archer grunted. "That's no problem. He just punches in a destination correction whenever we turn off the previous route. These things follow preset routes. You want to get crosstown, almost any destination over ten miles to the east of here, this car will follow the same route—or alternate route if traffic is getting heavy—up to a point. All he had to do is pick a destination way ahead of the general direction we're headed." The big man paused. "That's always assuming, of course, that he didn't have a manual override on the controls. But I don't suppose he would . . . too dangerous in this weather."

"Is that possible?" Frank asked.

"Anything's 'possible,' Frank. The only question is one of probabilities. However, just to set your mind at ease, I haven't spotted anyone obviously following us."

"I'm glad," Dorian said.

Their destination was in one of the backwater districts of Bristol Sector. Over the Cotwold Hills and to the north, near Malmesbury, the auto-taxi slid to a stop on a rain-slick cobbled street upon which timeless old brownstone row houses fronted. Archer led them up the steps to the nearest front door and touched a bell button.

They could hear nothing from within, and there was no immediate answer, but down in the street the auto-taxi, its running lights winking in the evening gloom, rolled quickly away. Then there were only the sounds of the rain.

Suddenly the door snapped open, a chain across it checking it only a few inches wide. A wrinkled face, wide blue eyes, and a topping of white hair peered around the door at them.

"Come on, now, Ronald," Archer said impatiently. "It's me. I've got a couple of young friends with me, and we're getting soaked out here. Let us in."

"Ah, Michael! Certainly, certainly. One moment, please, for the chain. One can't be too careful these days, you know. Can't be too careful."

The door slid shut again and something rattled on its other side. Then it opened wide. "Come in, come in," the old man said, standing aside.

He was certainly a remarkable looking man. In height, he towered over Archer (Frank was aghast at the name Michael, and didn't think Mike was much improvement; to him the cheerful big man would remain simply Archer), despite stooped shoulders. At one time the man must have been as big in girth as well, but now his big bones formed a framework from which the rest of his body was loosely slung. He wore a scarlet robe looking like a bathrobe, tied at the waist. And he bowed to them before shutting the door behind them.

"My oldest brother, Ronald Archer," Michael Archer said, introducing them. "He's dug himself into this cave in order to have a place to die, but I had the idea he might still be feeling lively enough to enjoy a few visitors."

"Ah, Michael, you're still a young rogue. What mischief are you up to now?" the old man said, smiling. He rubbed his hands together as if they were cold, but if anything the interior of the house was stiflingly warm.

"I'd like the opportunity to use a window, if I could," Archer replied. "I'd like to check the street."

They were standing in an old-fashioned hallway that made Frank wonder if this building might not actually date to his own era or earlier. The older Archer took a key from a pocket in his robe and unlocked a door opposite them. "Can't be too careful these days," he said over his shoulder. "I keep this whole floor locked up, as a rule." He let them into a musty room with shrouded furniture. Archer, *their* Archer, moved quickly to a front window, eased back a curtain, and peered out.

"Don't they have street lights on this block anymore, Ronald?" he asked in an irritated tone.

"Haven't, no, for the last two years. One of the signs, my boy. Deterioration. The area is in a bad way, you know."

"Yeah, I know. That's how you got this place so cheap. One of these days they'll take down the whole area and build it up again."

Ronald sighed. "I know. All that's stopped them are the Hills. I don't know which I dread the more—the advance of civilization or the decay of the area. Well, I shall be dead before the worst happens, I'm sure. I say—*is* there anyone out there?"

Archer had let the curtain fall back. "No," he said. "Not yet."

"We've wasted enough time," Archer said, leading them back into the hall. His brother locked the room behind them once more. "Ronald, where are you hiding your visi-set these days? You *do* still have a visi-set, I hope?"

The older man assumed a hurt look. "I'm not yet filing my bankruptcy papers, Michael," he said. "Of course, I still have the thing. Not that it isn't awfully expensive. You're not going to use it, are you? Calls cost me ten units now, you know, and I only get fifty units with the basic monthly charge."

"You haven't any friends," Archer said unkindly, "so you never make any calls. You can't begrudge us one call on your damned visi, can you? Not after we came all this way to use it?"

"I wondered why you'd come, Michael," his brother sighed. "Wouldn't it have been cheaper—not to mention easier—to use your own?"

"The set, Ronald," Archer said, threateningly. "The set!"

"Well, yes, of course; if you must insist!"

Frank found himself grinning at Dorian, who was still trying to keep a straight face.

Ronald Archer led them up the stairs to a sitting room. It was furnished with massively dark and ugly furniture, and even the two glow panels in the ceiling could not dispel its gloom.

"Good God, Ronald," Archer said. "You can't possibly *use* this room! The place looks like a crypt!"

While Frank agreed with him, he didn't say it when Ronald

Archer turned his gaze from his brother to Dorian and then to Frank, as though beseeching them for understanding.

"He *is* my *youngest* brother," Ronald Archer said, "so I'm sure we must all make our excuses for him." He went to the door. "I shall be downstairs if you want me; I'm going to dial a cup of stim-caff." The door closed behind him.

Archer sighed, shook his head, and then said, "Well, I guess I should make a few excuses for Ronald, too, but I won't. We've got more important business at hand.

"There are a number of ways we can play it," Archer said. "We can try for a local Syncom representative—an *official* rep, I mean—or we can make a direct call. It seems to me, a direct call would be simpler and quicker."

"Maybe I should make the call," Dorian said. "They'd recognize me."

"Good idea. You have the code?"

"I have my father's own private code."

"That's better yet."

"It ought to go right through to one of his own secretaries."

Archer sighed. Then he said, "Well, here it is. Go to it."

Dorian sat before the visi and began punching buttons. After a sequence that struck Frank as being longer than a zip code plus a Social Security number, the metallic finish of the panel faded into the glowing color screen. A bored face looked up.

"This is a private line. With whom did you wish to speak?"

The face was one, Dorian said later, she had seen before. She recalled no name to go with it, but it was not unfamiliar. "I want to talk to my father, My Lord Damon. This is Your Miss Dorian speaking." Her voice had taken on an autocratic tone.

The bored expression disappeared. In its place was sudden surprise, shock, and animation.

"Why, yes, of course—!"

And then, inexplicably, the screen went dead.

"What happened?" Dorian cried, swinging around to face Frank and Archer. "I'd gotten through! Why—?"

"Here, let me—" Archer said, leaning forward to push the emergency button.

The screen lit with a woman's face. *"Yes,"* she intoned, *"May*

I help you? What is your emergency, please?" It was a different face, but the words and tone were familiar.

"A call was placed from this set to New Delhi. It was interrupted; we were disconnected."

The woman's face jumped, as if her image had been videotaped and spliced at that point. *"What was the code for your call, please?"*

Archer gave it to her. Again the image jumped; her expression had altered slightly, her face was at a different angle. *"I'm sorry; that is not a working code."*

Archer snorted. "Okay, can you get us a working code?"

Another flicker. *"The code you request is not authorized for public listing."*

"Look, this is an emergency! We have to get through to that party. We had his personal code, and the call was broken, and now you say that code is no longer working. Well, we're not the public, and since we had the right code, I think you'd better give us a working alternate code." Archer spoke in controlled tones, as though addressing a willful child.

"I'm sorry, but that is not a function of this code. This is an emergency code. If you have no emergency, please disconnect."

The screen frosted over with silver as it went blank. Archer delivered himself of several well-rounded curses without apologizing to Dorian.

"Those idiot computers," he said at last, "have all the intelligence of a backward three-year-old."

"That was a computer?" Frank asked.

"Yeah, they just have a woman read off all the possible replies they deem necessary, and record them for the circuits. Then when you call, they can talk to you as if the computer was human."

"She didn't hear us?" Dorian asked.

"Nope. The computer heard us, though. And it selected the proper prerecorded response. Such as it was . . ."

"What can we do now?" Frank asked.

"Try again," Archer said. "Since the fast way didn't work, we'll try the slow way—via the local offices of Syncom." He began punching in a fresh code.

The screen did not light.

Archer growled to himself. He punched the red emergency button again.

Nothing happened. The visi was dead.

The big man straightened up, squaring his shoulders. "Okay," he said. "So we made a mistake. It wasn't a total mistake; at least your father will know you're alive. But . . ." he shrugged. "Come on. We've got to get moving."

"What's happening?" Frank asked, as he ran after Archer. He had Dorian's hand and was pulling her after him down the stairs.

"My stupidity," Archer said. "Transystems was monitoring calls. Not outgoing calls from any particular locality—incoming calls at Syncom's end. Bet there's a real fuss going on there right now."

"But—"

"Yeah, our set went dead, too. Well, that means they've back-traced us, and we haven't a lot of time left."

"What's all this, Michael?" Ronald asked, looking up from the foot of the stairs. He was holding a cup in his hand which steamed with a rich aroma that Frank at once identified as coffee. "What's happening? Have you broken my visi?"

"Nope," Archer said. He reached into the pocket of Ronald's robe, took out a key, and unlocked the front room again. His voice came back into the hall. "You got a back exit from this place, Ronald?"

"Why?"

"Because the street is filling up with cars, and I don't want to get run down by one of them."

"What's that you say? Cars in the street?"

"Look for yourself. But answer my question."

Ronald ran into the room, Frank and Dorian behind him. He shouldered his brother aside, took one horrified look from the window, and asked, "But, what do they all *want?*"

"Us," Archer said. "Now let's get going!"

"Michael, I'm sorry," Ronald said, ducking his head and staring at the floor. "Last year; it was last year I had an attempted break-in, and, well, I sealed off the back way."

The bell rang.

Chapter Sixteen

FRANK STARED, TRANSFIXED, AS THE two brothers faced each other, Archer glaring, Ronald paling. He thought for a minute Archer would hit the older man.

"How well do you have this place fortified, Ronald?" the younger brother asked in an ominously quiet voice.

"Eh, well, very well, I should hope. I—I'm afraid we couldn't get at the back way anymore. Had it bricked up, you see. . . ."

The bell sounded again. It rang from somewhere up above, on the second floor.

"How long do you think the front door will hold?"

"Oh, quite well, I should think." Ronald moved into the hallway and fingered a switch. Immediately a concealed second door, of thick, flat, featureless gray metal, slid across the doorway.

"How about the windows?" Archer asked sardonically.

"Same thing," his brother replied, and touched another switch. Heavy metal plates slid up from below the floor to meet the ceiling, completely covering the inside of the windows.

"Well, that must've tipped them off," Archer said. "They can't miss that." The bell had stopped ringing. "Too bad we can't see out anymore. Be interesting to see what they try next."

"Ah, Michael, I have a thought."

"And what might that be? To call the security squad on your

dead visi?" It was the first time Frank had seen the big man so visibly annoyed.

"The roof," Ronald said. "You might try the roof. It connects, I believe, with the roofs of the houses on both sides. It's a flat roof, you know—just a little slant on it. Slants back, from the front; ought to offer some cover from below, eh?"

Archer's face broke into a grin. He clapped his brother on the shoulder, half staggering the older man. "Now, that's an idea, huh?" he said. "Okay, let's not waste any more time at this."

"What about *me?*" Ronald asked. "What shall I *do?*"

"Wait till we're gone, then let them in, of course!" Archer said. "Be yourself! You're guilty of nothing. You're just a law-abiding citizen who's afraid of burglars in the night. Oh—you might complain about your visi going dead. You tried to call the security squad."

Other people were also moving, in other places in the world.

In the Indian mountain palace of Syncom, a frantic staff was coping with both the effects of a bomb in the communications center —the palace's main link with the outer world—and the news that the kidnapped Heiress Dorian was still alive, and had been traced to a point between the fifty-first and fifty-second parallels, not far west of the zero meridian, a point within the Megapolis of England. Or at least that her call had originated its broadcast at that point, according to the Syncom satellite which had handled it. The local exchange was no longer traceable, and, in any case, was not a Syncom exchange.

In a deceptively spacious room one mile beneath the California Sierras, an old man stared at a private-linkage visi-screen and listened with an impassive face while a man reported to him of developments and played for him a recording of Dorian's call to Syncom. The old man did not move, but when he spoke, many others moved quickly.

And out on the street, in front of Ronald Archer's house, a group of men swarmed from their cars while neighbors drew their shades tighter, and retreated from the sight. One of the men set up a machine on a tripod before the door, and began burning the door down.

"They've set the house afire!" Ronald said agitatedly. "I can smell it—wood's burning!"

127

"Sit tight, Ronald," Archer said. "It's probably just the front door. See you again sometime, and—thanks!"

The big man dropped the trapdoor shut again, his fingers wet and grimy from where he'd held it. He wiped his hands and then, crouching over, he led them across the roof to the next house.

They were back in the fantasy again. Frank's heart hammered heavily but in another part of his mind, removed and distant, he could not accept this chase across rooftops, anymore than he had the earlier attempts on their lives. It was unreal, the stuff of lurid spy movies, *a fantasy*.

But the slippery tiled roof under his feet was real, and the aching pain in his side, and so was the fine mist that cut into his face, and Archer's muffled curses when the man found the trapdoor to the next house closed and locked. There was only a vague sort of light, reflected from the mist droplets in the air, its origins lost. A grayness that faded into blackness; Archer and Dorian two unequal shapes looming ahead.

Each roof was bisected by a low wall where the buildings met, and often the roofs were of unequal heights. He stumbled and moved on, taking care not to lose his footing. They were three stories up, and there was no wall at the low side of the roofs—only a killing fall.

Then he heard Archer's pleased grunt, and the next moment he was following Dorian down steep dark stairs while Archer lowered the trapdoor back down in place behind them.

An old couple lived in the house with their two sons and their sons' families. Archer had to hit the bigger son before he established his authority over them. Then he was permitted to call Local Security on the visi and to inform them that a gang was breaking into the house of Ronald Archer. That news seemed almost as unsettling to the assembled families as had been the abrupt descent into the house by the three strangers.

Archer debated aloud the odds in favor of trying for the local Syncom office, and then decided against it. "Everything going there is being monitored, now. The enemy knows we're here. We'd best just move on."

The back door of the old house opened on a bricked courtyard and a neat garden. Archer led the way across the garden and over the dividing fence into the adjoining backyard of the house across the way. Frank helped Dorian over the fence, and then scrambled over after her, all the while trying to concentrate upon the immediate, ignoring the possible—well, probable—outcome of their flight.

In an age of instant communications, everything could happen too quickly. Halfway around the world, a computer could take a single nanosecond to reach its decision, and instantly the world could collapse around them. They were outflanked by the vast communication intersystems built up by rival corporations. The best they could hope for was momentary escape, and then to escape again. Archer could no longer shield them—he'd become identified with them now, and his I.D. in an auto-taxi slot or public visi would trigger Transystems monitors as quickly as could the sight of Dorian's face or the sound of her name.

But Archer was still the man in charge, still a man Frank would trust. If anyone could pull them through this, it would be Archer.

The only occupant of the house beyond the backyard they'd crossed was an attractive young woman lying on a filthy bed, amid piles of litter and garbage, a stim-box wire attached to her temple. She opened her eyes and stared at them in an unfocused way. The beginnings of a frown appeared on her forehead, but her fingers closed reflexively around the little black box, and the frown was erased by a sleepy smile as her eyes closed again.

Archer shook his head wearily, but shooed both Frank and Dorian out of the room.

"But, she needs help," Dorian protested.

"She chose her path a long time ago," Archer said, and his disapproval was written plainly on his face. He reentered the woman's room and closed her door firmly behind him.

"What's he going to do with her?" Dorian asked.

"I don't know," Frank said.

"What's—why does she have one of those ugly black boxes?" Dorian wanted to know. From inside the room came the muffled sounds of slapping, and a querulous voice.

"Instant happiness," Frank said, drawing her away from the door. He had a strong suspicion of the woman's social standing, and could guess her need for the stim-box. But—what did Archer want with her? "I guess some things don't change that much. Used

129

to be, a woman like her would get drunk or use drugs. These stim-box things are more efficient, I guess."

The door slid open, and Archer was supporting the woman. "But . . . I just want to be left *alone,*" the woman was saying.

"Look on it as a straight business transaction," Archer said, leading her across the hall and into a smaller, tiled room. The door shut behind them again.

Frank shrugged. "Don't ask me," he said.

When the door was open again, the woman's hair was brushed back and her clothes smoothed out a bit. "—But I don't *have* a visi," she was protesting.

"But you've got a taxi callbox, haven't you?" Archer said. "You *must* have."

She nodded.

"Good. Then you know what you're going to do."

"You're going to get me into trouble," she said, but she didn't seem to be trying very hard now. "They'll trace me."

Archer signaled Frank and Dorian to follow him down the stairs, and spoke soothingly to the woman. "Nonsense. We won't use *your* I.D. in the slot. And if anyone should ever ask, we were just a couple of Johns. Right?"

"Well, I don't know. . . ."

Frank felt a tingle of alarm. If Archer wasn't using the woman's I.D., then he would have to use his own! But that was no longer safe. Transystems was sure to be monitoring all taxi calls from this area, and certain to know Archer's I.D. code by now. Once it had gone into their eidetic computer memory banks, it could be keyed into instant rocognition by any of their monitoring taps—legal or illegal. And there hardly seemed any question now of Transystems' scruples over legality.

But Archer seemed to know what he was doing, and the I.D. card he thrust into the taxi callbox summoned only an auto-taxi —no one else.

The taxi took the four of them to the Trowbridge District, some distance south. There, in a public visi-booth, Archer settled the woman, bent over her to whisper some last-minute instruction, and then thrust an I.D. card into the call-slot.

The screen lit with a man's haggard features. *"Yes,"* he said.

"Syncom Bristol; what is it?" He looked irritated at the interruption of the call.

"I'd, uh, I'd like to speak, umm, with the local rep—the chief Bristol Syncom rep, I mean," the young woman said nervously.

"You are. What is it, madam? I'm busy."

If the chief local representative was answering the visi, Frank realized with a start, *all his men must be busy in the field. Dorian's call must've stirred up a hornet's nest!*

Speaking quickly, the woman spoke her brief rehearsed message. "Transystems kidnapped Dorian," she said.

Immediately Archer reached over her shoulder for the disconnect button. "Okay, that's it. Let's get moving." They piled back into the waiting auto-taxi.

It was a simple plan. Transystems was desperate to keep all knowledge of its role in the kidnapping secret. Necessarily, secrecy militantly enforced meant killing those who knew the secrets.

But if the facts of the kidnapping were known . . . ?

It was that simple. Transystems would have nothing further to gain by any continued efforts to silence the trio.

Archer had rehearsed the hesitant woman thoroughly. "Remember, the first word is 'Transystems.' No matter what, you'll get that much through. If you can say 'Transystems kidnapped—,' that much and no more, you've told them the most important facts. If you get the chance for 'Transystems kidnapped Dorian,' you've said it all. But even that single word, 'Transystems,' will point the finger in the right direction. Syncom won't be stupid about it. They'll put the sums together and reach the right answer."

Somewhere under the high Sierras, an old man listened impassively to the report. They'd torn it, now. Damn and blast the idiocy of underlings and the conspiracy of fate! He hadn't ordered the kidnapping of the girl, and he hadn't wanted it. It had been presented to him, *fait accompli,* by the machinations of chance and stupidity working hand in hand. He wanted no part of it. Once it had been brought to him the best he could hope for was to wash his hands of it, quickly. He'd planned hastily, improvising: Two men had been involved in the kidnapping who knew the facts. Have one disposed of. Have the second dispose of the evidence. Destroy him.

Nothing had worked right. Somehow, the man entrusted to do

the job had been too canny; he'd sealed a recording of his instructions with Intrabank. It had taken over eighteen hours to break the man down, retrieve the recording, and destroy them both. And during that time, his coordination of incoming information had been lax. It had taken him more than a day to key in the security-officer report on his own computer and realize the two children were still alive. He hadn't wanted to believe that. He'd sent for the visi-recording for his own viewing. Two of them: a boy and Heiress Dorian. He recognized *her* well enough. Somewhere in Ellay . . . hours ago. Could have gone anywhere, since. The boy was that time-traveler, no doubt. He'd forgotten the boy. Intelligence reports turned in since the kidnapping verified the fact that Syncom had gotten nothing of value from the boy.

All this incredible entanglement out of a pointless piece of corporate espionage, a needless kidnapping!

But there had still been time to pick up the pieces. The damage had been done, but thus far Transystems' name had not been involved in it. Thank God for the monitors he'd ordered on Syncom communications! He'd gotten those into effect immediately.

But nothing worked right. "What a tangled web we weave. . . ." the words ran meaninglessly through his mind, over and over. The children had confederates, had picked them up Lord knew where. . . . A Michael Archer, once with DelVaCo, briefly of Transystems . . . a malcontent, minor troublemaker. If he ever came back to his home in Nevada Territory, he'd live to regret it. Ronald Archer, older brother, living in Open Territory . . . no problem there. He could be taken care of. And a minor piece of filth who called himself Victor Jerrold these days . . . he'd had other names in the past; tomorrow he'd be a statistic in the death tables.

But all that didn't matter now.

Syncom knew.

They'd gotten through; *Syncom knew.*

Sitting alone in his mile-deep cavern bunker, the old man knew real fear for the first time in his life. He raised his hand to thumb a switch, and his hand shook. Rock-steady, that hand had always been.

How soon would Syncom move?

He thought of Lord Damon, and wondered, *Is he the impetuous type, or will he choose to lie and wait?* A cold, hard man, he'd always thought him, but where his daughter was concerned, an unknown factor.

A sound rustled from behind him, startling him.

Now? Here? Like this?

Apprehension poured adrenalin into his system; his heart leapt and he felt the blood leave his head momentarily as he came swiftly to his feet and turned.

Something . . . else . . .

Blackness flooded his mind; he folded up and fell.

His servant, Dextor, found him thus, as he rushed forward with the forgotten luncheon platter still in his hands.

The Old Man was dead. His heart had stopped.

Chapter Seventeen

FRANK SAT QUIETLY BESIDE DORIAN, her hand in his. Her hand felt warm, confident, comforting. And the oblique shocked glances of the local Syncom rep couldn't take that away.

He felt terribly alone.

"We'll be perfectly safe in here until your father's men come, My Miss Dorian," the rep had told them. He spoke to Dorian, trying his best to ignore Frank. "The place is sealed like a fortress."

They had a direct line to Syncom from here, one that no one could cut. Dorian had sat before the visi-screen and spoken to her father, whose stern visage faced her. Frank had stayed to one side, in the background, hoping he wouldn't be noticed.

He should've gone with Archer.

His stomach was knotted with the tension, and in a grim way that amused him: All he'd gone through, and *now* he was scared!

Dorian squeezed his hand. "I know it will work out all right," she said. "Daddy will have to fix things for you."

He glanced at her, wondering if she realized how much she had changed since their first meeting. His stomach clenched again.

"Good-bye, kid," Archer had said. *"Good luck. And—you know where to find me . . . if you need to."*

The big man's hand had engulfed his, had squeezed lightly and released it. Then the taxi door had slammed shut and its tires were squealing on the wet pavement. *Gone.*

Archer was gone. He missed the man already. There was this, well, call it *presence,* to the big man. It wasn't just his size, although that was part of it, certainly. It was that his personality was as big as his body. He had drive, warmth, and an aura of unfailing competence.

"I miss him too," Dorian said, breaking the silence with a whisper. She was reading his mind. "I wish he'd come with us."

"You two are all set, now," Archer had told them. *"You'll be home free, soon. You don't need me anymore."* He'd given them a rather lopsided grin, and a chuckle. *"We pulled through,"* he said. He held up an I.D. card. *"You can thank Mr. Jerrold for that."* It had been Jerrold's I.D. that had summoned the auto-taxi, and paid for the visi-call. Poetic justice?

"He didn't want to get involved," Frank said.

"But, we could've gotten him a good job, a high position," Dorian said.

"He never let us thank him," Frank said. Inside him a dormant memory stirred: He'd distrusted Archer—and never really had the chance to make it up to the man. Now he never would.

"He could have let us help him," Dorian said, a little wistfully.

"I think he'd rather live out in that desert, on top of that mesa, away from people," Frank replied.

"Are you sorry you didn't go with him?" she asked.

"A little," he said. He looked at her. "Everything's going to be okay for you, now. I'm not so sure it will work out as well for me."

"Then why are you coming?" she demanded, her voice a little hurt.

"You," he said. "I guess I'm not ready yet to say good-bye."

An airbus took them to the rocket pad in southern Ireland Territory, an official part of the Megapolis of England and the Open Territory, but underpopulated, its green hills and downs little changed for a thousand years, to say nothing of the last five hundred.

There they boarded a private suborbital rocket, emblazoned with the personal shield of Damon of Syncom. Armed guards surrounded them, but there were no incidents. Transystems might just as well have forgotten them.

They were strapped into luxurious couches. Like the pneumobeds, these couches seemed filled with a liquid that adjusted itself

135

to their weight. But unlike the beds, these couches wrapped themselves around each occupant in a way that cushioned every part of the body.

Ports were closed. Frank's ears snapped as the internal pressure system came into play. Everything was very quiet. The cabin of the rocket was long enough to seat forty passengers. There were only six, Frank and Dorian and four guards. It semed like an awful waste.

A distant noise began, and Frank felt the air around him vibrate. The couch held him quite motionless. Then it thrust itself up against him, enfolding him into itself, lifting, holding, surrounding him. The noise and the vibrations went away. The pressure ceased.

He turned his head and looked at Dorian, across the narrow aisle. It reminded him of the trip on the San Bernardino Express. He wondered if the rocket had been delayed, if the engines had been cut off. *Could Transystems—?*

"We're on our way," Dorian said softly. "The last leg of the trip."

"We'll be at apogee in seven minutes," a man's voice spoke from behind them. "It'll be a short trip."

"Any shorter and we'd have been forced to go around the other way," another man snorted. Then, as if realizing they were speaking in the company of an Heir, they said no more.

It was hard to realize that he was taking a rocket flight outside the Earth's atmosphere. This, at last, was a genuine taste of tomorrow! This was the trip he'd dreamed of as a small boy, watching the teevee space operas and thrilling to the notion of real space travel. The astronauts—this was what they'd pioneered, this was what some of them had given their lives for. A soundless cabin and a less than twenty-minute flight.

At apogee the rocket reached the top of its trajectory, and turned, swapping tail for nose, to fall once again for the planet below. And in those long moments of free fall, as they coasted up and over the top and down again, only the restraining straps held Frank in his couch, and only determination held the last meal he'd eaten in his stomach.

He was falling—!

Every nerve in his body screamed the warning. His muscles

knotted, tense against the impact. His stomach squeezed into a tiny ball and nausea washed over him.

He gripped tightly to the arms of the couch, telling himself grimly that he would not fall, he would not be hurt. He was weightless, and his instincts knew only one explanation for that. But his mind, his intellect, knew another, and held hold of it as tightly as his hands did the couch.

"Frank? You—all right?"

He turned his head again, brain whirling, inner ears tumbling, balance destroyed, and felt a fresh spasm of nausea. He managed a weak smile. "Yeah, I think so. How about you?"

Dorian returned his smile. "I feel fine, but you look a little green."

"I guess so," was all he could reply.

Then, gradually, weight began returning. His stomach retreated from his chest, and somewhere inside of him order was regained, *down* and *up* were reestablished. He felt weak and relieved.

And all too soon after that, the rocket had thundered tail first down to a landing.

He'd been right in his apprehensions—it wasn't going to work out like it did in the books, with a happy ending.

He'd followed Dorian down from the rocket into the elevator, the four guards surrounding them, and stepped out into the bright Indian sun. It glared on the white field, blurring the scattered black radial streaks of heat scars. When the men surrounded them he was separated from Dorian so swiftly and easily that he had hardly time to catch his breath before she was hustled into a waiting car. Men moved him purposefully into another car, and this second car did not follow the first.

They held something to his arm that tingled, and he blacked out. The next he knew for certain—there were flashes of other fleeting memories, but they might have been dreams—he was sitting in a chair, his head and body wired, and a brooding Damon sat across the small room facing him.

The room was darkened, and he was surrounded by a pool of bright light. Damon's face and hands were pale in the reflected light, his body invisible.

"You despoiled my daughter," the man said, biting out each

word from between his teeth. Damon was, Frank, slowly realized, holding back a primal rage.

He tried to shake his head, but it was clamped in place. "No," he said. "No, I didn't."

"You aided in her kidnapping and you seduced her," the implacable Lord Damon stated.

"I didn't! *Ask* her," Frank cried out.

"I've spoken with my daughter. You've seduced at least her mind. And now we'll see about the rest." Damon nodded to someone standing behind the big chair, and Frank heard movement.

What followed was a nightmare.

It made his previous session with the memory-probe seem almost a vacation by comparison. That time they had wanted only a few seconds of his memories. Now they wanted days.

He had no knowledge of the extent of the passage of time. It was impossible to tell. Did every minute he relived for them take a real minute of time? Or could they speed him up over the unimportant parts, as easily as they'd slowed him down to examine those few seconds before? He had no watch, and his inner clock had been disconnected. Perhaps it took only a few hours—perhaps it took a week.

He would surface from time to time, aware that the machine had been shut off for some purpose, but it seemed to have nothing to do with him, and he would fall quickly asleep in the interval. Then his memories would return, nightmares, to reawaken him.

They had attached a tube to his arm, other plumbing to his lower body. Like an organic unit in a machine, he was fed nutriments directly into his veins, and his wastes were automatically removed. He was being serviced purely because of the necessity to keep him alive for the duration of the recording of his memories—not out of any misplaced humanitarian instincts on the part of his captors.

Then at last he fell asleep to remain asleep.

"Young man, you are most fortunate to be alive. Please don't complain to me about your lot."

The man looked like a saint, his expression warm, kindly, his eyes twinkling, his head wreathed with a halo of white floss. Frank hated him.

It was easy to hate Albert, as it was easy to hate every employee of Syncom.

"Get off it, you old hypocrite," Frank said bitterly. "My good fortune was to get out of this place alive, and to stay alive out there. I wish I'd never come back."

It was a full circle. They'd even put him back in his old room in the tower—or one exactly like it. It would be hard to tell the difference. The window was covered by metal shutters.

"You came back of your own choosing," Albert chided him.

"Sure; thinking maybe Dorian's father had an ounce of decency to him, thinking maybe he'd be grateful to me for getting Dorian back alive and safe."

"There seems to be doubt about that last."

"What a bunch of filthy minds you all are!" Frank shouted. "You stole all my memories from me, took them all down on tape, and for all I know you play them over for kicks twice a day. So you know as well as I do everything that went on between me and Dorian."

"You come from a barbaric age," the saintly old man said gently. "Why should anyone believe you did not take advantage of the girl?"

"How much proof do you *need,* for Christ's sake?" Frank asked. He leapt to his feet and began pacing back and forth. "Are you all so corrupt and decadent you can't imagine a guy like me might have a little respect for a girl as innocent as Dorian? Don't you think I didn't have my thoughts sometimes—but I'll bet plenty you've had some of your own, you old fool!"

Albert colored, and looked uncomfortable for the first time.

"There's no need to indulge in language of that sort," he said reprovingly.

"The fact is," Frank continued, "I think I fell in love with the girl. Does that shake you up so badly?"

"No," replied Albert, "but the fact that she reciprocates—now, that's cause for alarm."

"Why, dammit?" Frank shouted. He ignored the inner voice that said, *She does?*

"Why? My dear boy, My Miss Dorian is an *Heir.* How can you forget this? She is an Heir, and you are not. It is that simple."

139

"Big deal," Frank muttered. "An accident of birth."

Albert raised his voice angrily. "There is *no* accident to birth, young man, and I'll thank you not to forget it! She is an Heir, and one of a bloodline that does not mix with the mainstream—and most assuredly not with mongrels," he snapped.

"But she loves me," Frank said, softly, to himself.

"She's infatuated with you. A fixation, quite adolescent, the product of her cherished innocence, her lack of previous exposure to your kind. Nothing more. It will not interfere with the wedding."

"The wedding? *What* wedding?"

"Why, to Elton of Transystems, of course," the white-haired little old man said.

Chapter Eighteen

FRANK FELT STUNNED, SUDDENLY CONFUSED.

"But—Elton . . . Transystems . . . they tried to have her *killed!*"

Albert waved his hand, brushing away an imaginary fly. "That is done and past," he said composedly.

" 'Done and past'?" Frank echoed unbelievingly. "Now I've heard it all! Are your lot so damned callous that you can forget what they did, *that fast?*"

Albert sighed. "I truly wonder why I put up with your continued abuse," he wheezed.

"Well, why do you?"

"But the fact of the matter is that I am here to inform you of certain things. And principal among them is this: Elton's father is dead."

"The Old Man? The head of Transystems?"

"The Old Man made the decision on this personally," the copter pilot had said, before he dumped them into the ocean. *The Old Man himself:* Elton's father, the head of the gigantic network that was called Transystems. *He was the one who ordered us killed.*

Albert nodded. "Died of a heart attack. Stupid man, for an Heir, I mean. He was overdue a new heart for months."

What made Heirs such superior beings? When they died, they

were just as dead. *And while they lived, they could be just as stupid!*

"So now it's all just as if it had never happened, huh?" Frank said. "Dorian is home safe and the game is over."

"Well, let us say not exactly," Albert smiled. "There are certain advantages accruing to Syncom's present situation. We have the recordings of your memories, for instance. They would not constitute binding legal proof, but they are sufficient to gain leverage over Transystems and its new and younger management. And I can assure you that the forthcoming marriage will improve our position." Albert had the look of a well-fed cat washing its paws.

"Why tell me all this?" Frank demanded. "What's it to me?"

"Why tell you?" Albert repeated. "Well, one might expect you to be a little pleased at the fortunate way in which your adventure has turned out, if, of course, a little disgruntled at your inability to leap into the status of Heir for yourself. Remember, as the Roman philosopher Plato once put it, 'A cat may look at a king, but a dog can never become a prince.' "

Frank snorted. "Boy, you're the complete phony, aren't you? Plato never said anything like that."

"Then, too," Albert continued, "there is this: In appreciation for your role in returning My Miss Dorian, her father has decided to grant you his supreme favor."

"What's that? Permission to breathe air for another twenty-four hours?" Frank asked sarcastically.

"He proposes to return you to your own time."

The room was like a cell, especially since they'd done that to the windows, closing them off. He sat down on the bed, stood up again, paced, threw himself spread-eagle on the bed, squirmed, rolled over and jumped off again, and paced some more.

He knew where the light switch was now, but he couldn't turn it off; he couldn't lie down; he couldn't sleep.

He remembered again the smug look on old Albert's face as the man had told him about their plans for him. "They want back their star-drive. At the moment, unless all calculations are off, it is occupying the place where you last stood in your backyard. And, of course, despite the way you've poisoned young Dorian's mind against him, My Lord Damon does bear you much gratitude."

"So they're going to try to swap me back for their machine?"

Frank had asked, not knowing whether he dared believe the man.

"Nobody really knows anything about time-travel," Albert had mused to himself. "The question of temporal parity is a moot point—unasked, unanswered. What happens when you displace two objects in time? Does the, eh, 'swap' maintain the balance, or are subtly resonating cosmic forces set up to disturb the fabric of space-time? Dear me, I have no idea. And neither has anyone else, of course. But it does make sense to try to return everything to its previous state of equilibrium."

"So when you come right down to it," Frank had jibed, "it has nothing to do with gratitude."

"My boy, you'd best watch that tongue of yours. I'm sure that if Damon was pressed he could find another your size, weight, and shape," Albert had said, rising at last from his chair. He folded the chair and tucked it under his arm, thumbed open the door, and closed it behind him. His last words were, "Tomorrow morning, then."

The door didn't respond to Frank's efforts; it had obviously been locked from outside.

Tomorrow morning?

Home?

He couldn't sleep. He was restless, he fidgeted, he paced, his heart hammered, and his mind raced.

He felt as he hadn't in years. Remember when you were only six, and Christmas day grew closer at a snail's pace? The days dragged by interminably, and then at last Christmas Eve was here, and you had only to sleep a single night before Christmastime? And you couldn't sleep? The moon shone brightly in your window, and you'd sit bolt upright in bed and stare around your room and out the window—perhaps at a blanket of white snow, or the naked, skeletal branches of a tree. Your watch, your prized watch with the numerals that glowed in the dark—the watch you fell on and broke two years later in a scuffle at recess—you stared at the hands that pointed to 1:30 and wondered how much longer you'd have to wait. Could you get up at 5:30? Or maybe 5:00? And what would you find in your stocking, hung from a chairback because your house had no mantel? Your heart beat faster in anticipation, and when you dozed off again it was to dream a thousand fragments of dreams in which, yes, you did indeed get up to get your stocking—only to wake up each time,

143

squint at your watch, and lie back down again, to wait and doze some more. . . .

Home.

The most precious gift of all.

He'd been sick with the wanting, and yet certain that he would never see his time and home again. And then he'd met Archer, and had a real friend in this world, and it hadn't been so bad. And Dorian . . . when he'd still had that wistful hope that Hollywood movie endings *weren't* impossible . . . when he'd known how she felt about him and hoped that maybe . . .

He kicked at the wall, stubbing his toe. Then he switched off the light and threw himself again on the bed.

Somehow he dozed off. . . .

The light from the opening door jarred him awake. In the darkness of the room the light was a bright square that outlined a figure. He blinked his eyes, then knuckled them. Someone stood silhouetted in the doorway, staring at him.

A dream . . . or a memory of the past?

The door closed, and then a soft glow came from the ceiling.

"Dorian," he whispered. He wondered in his confusion if it had all been a dream—their kidnapping, escape, and adventures together . . . The heavy cloak of *déjà vu* settled down over his shoulders. "What are you doing here?" he asked, and the words echoed in his mind. *This has all happened before.*

Then the pattern was broken. Dorian came swiftly to the bedside and knelt beside him. "Frank," she whispered, "are you all right?"

Her eyes were directly opposite his. He stared into them, and he wondered if he had ever really looked at this girl before.

"You—you shouldn't be here," he said at last.

"I know. But . . . Frank, they're sending you back, tomorrow, aren't they? Albert told me."

"Yeah, that's what he told me, too."

"Are you glad?"

He shrugged. "Yeah, I guess so."

"It had to work out this way, I guess," she said.

"They explained it all to you? About still marrying Elton, and everything?"

"Yes." She lowered her eyes.

"It's all for the good of the corporation, right?"

"That's what they said."

"After all," Frank found himself saying, "Elton never knew . . . about everything, I mean."

"Oh, Frank," Dorian sobbed, throwing herself against him, "I hate him!"

"Who? Elton?"

"Elton—Albert—my father . . . I hate them all!"

"I guess it's like Archer said—you have to learn to live with things as they are." He ran his fingers through her short hair, stroking it. She cuddled against him.

"The people—all the real people out there, they hate us, don't they? All us Heirs, I mean."

He shrugged again, feeling his shoulders move against the yielding bed. "I guess they do."

"And they're right, too, aren't they?"

Frank felt his own anger wash out of him. He felt very tired and much older. *This* is what he'd done to Dorian—he'd taken her innocence about herself and the rest of the world away from her. In only a handful of days, she'd learned more about the real world in which she lived than she had in all her previous life.

There's innocence, and then there's innocence. There's an open kind of naïveté that bespeaks the essential goodness in a person —and there's a simple blindness or ignorance to the reality of the world. He'd left the first intact, but the second was forever shattered, gone. But that had been a necessary product of her first real education. She lived in a world that was hopelessly corrupt, a world in which, through the marvels of modern science, the wielders of power held the rest of mankind in subtle slavery.

There was nothing new about it, save one thing: It was planet-wide; indeed, system-wide. There was no escape.

The perfect city-state of the ancient Greeks? Built on slave labor, it was not so different from the world Syncom controlled. At the top, the hereditary aristocrats. Below them, the freemen, the merchant and managerial class. And at the bottom, the slaves.

Thanks to the wonders of modern science, slaves weren't necessary anymore—not for raw labor. Machines were available. But the rest of the structure remained. And they had the gall to call it

145

"true" democracy! How can a man know freedom, when some computer, somewhere in the world or on another world, always knows where he is, at every instant? Freedom was always an illusion, a way of walking the common paths so that one never bumped into the fences and walls that abridged true freedom, and one could forget they were there. And necessarily so, for true freedom is chaos, where any man may attack any other man for his possessions, or even strike him dead for crossing his path. If two men are to share the same world, freedom must have its commonly agreed limits.

But no one had agreed to the limits imposed upon the people of this world. There were no options. Archer, living atop his desert mesa, enjoyed an illusion of privacy but was no more "free" than any other citizen whose I.D. was programmed into half a dozen computer banks daily as he rode to work, bought his meals, or paid his rent.

No wonder the space explorers to other systems had never returned! Theirs was the only true escape.

And tomorrow Frank would trade himself for a machine which, when perfected, might carry this system of oppression to the far stars. . . .

Balance your own selfish life against such a fate for mankind, and what is your decision? *Well, after all, they can still do it without that particular hunk of hardware, and* I want to go home.

And so the girl and the boy lay side by side on the narrow bed in the late hours of the night, and they talked softly to each other, for each was acutely aware that this would almost certainly be their last time together.

"Frank? Do you love me?"

"Yes," he said. "I think so."

"I never . . . loved anyone before:"

"Me neither. I thought I did, but . . . well, I guess I didn't."

"It's all so crazy, so wrong!" she wept. "I wish I could sneak into the lab and go back with you. . . ."

He tightened his arms around her. "You can't. You know they wouldn't let you."

"I know. Tomorrow I must begin rehearsals for the wedding." Her voice was bitter.

"This is your place, I guess," he said. "This is where you have to be."

146

"If I was a, a common, ordinary person, I could get a, what did they call it, a temporary contract? With you, I mean. Would you stay if I got one?" She was playing a game, he realized, a game of make-believe. And she was coaxing him to play it with her. They both knew he couldn't stay, now that her father had decided to send him back, and they both knew she couldn't play at being one of the lowborn and get a temporary contract.

But, "Yes," he told her softly. "I would stay."

"I knew you would!" She snuggled up against him, happy to cuddle close to him like this. She nibbled at his neck.

In the silence that followed, he wondered to himself what it might be like if they really could do such a thing. What kind of a wife would she make him? And how good a husband would he be? He'd seen some teen-aged marriages before. There was Larry Cohn, who married Linda Olsen when they were both juniors in high school. It hadn't been a "forced" marriage; they'd been going steady ever since junior high and just plain decided to make it permanent and legal. Funny, the way they both changed after that. Larry wasn't much fun to be around anymore, and he and Linda didn't spend much of their common schooltime together. And just this summer their folks put in for the annulment.

Kids, playing at being grown-ups.

It was just a game, until they'd both realized it was for real. Then it was over.

Dorian was crying.

"It's all so *wrong*," she sobbed. "It shouldn't have to end this way!"

He tried to hold her and soothe her, gently stroking her back and suddenly feeling like a protective older brother. "It has to be, that's all. Our liking or not liking it just doesn't make any difference. We're just tiny cogs on the wheels of corporation politics. What gets done to us is what's expedient."

She sniffled. "I know. I've heard it all from my father, from Albert, even from Gam'ma. I know why it's all happening . . . but I don't have to like it."

"Part of growing up is learning to do things you don't like," he said. *Boy, was that ever a standard platitude!* How many times had Mr. Helpern told him that? *"That's part of accepting responsibility,"* the psychologist would say, as if "responsibility" was an un-

147

pleasant chore, something you wanted to avoid. *Responsibility was learning to care for someone—helping her to accept her own role in life.*

"You know," he continued, "you are probably the first Heir in a hundred years who's seen much of the real outside world. You know that? You're the first Heir who knows what it's like, *not* to be an Heir. That ought to be worth something, you see what I mean?"

"You mean, I could maybe help do something, help make changes?" she asked.

"Well, maybe not very big changes, not right away. But, well, think about it: You'll have kids someday—"

"Never! I never want to get close to that Elton!"

"Well, if you *do* have kids, someday, you can help educate them, you know. You don't have to leave it all up to snobbish tutors. You could even—hey, listen to this: You could even send your kids out, in regular people-type clothes, to wander around the real world, just the way *we* did, so they'd learn it all firsthand! Like a snowball: Start it rolling and it keeps getting bigger. Your kids have their own kids, and . . . well, after awhile, a lot of them might be able to do things. After all, responsibility goes with power, you know. And maybe if they really knew what they were *doing* to people, well, maybe . . ."

"It's a beautiful dream, isn't it?" she whispered.

"Yes. And maybe nothing more."

But it was a seed, and maybe planting it now was a fair trade for the machine he'd change places with tomorrow, the machine that would eventually give mankind the stars.

There are a lot of stars out there. These people won't be able to hold them all.

"It's late, isn't it?" Dorian said.

"Must be early morning."

"Soon you'll be gone," she said, "as though you never were." Tears ran freely down her face and onto his.

The door snicked open suddenly and Frank was snapped into abrupt wakefulness as the lights glowed brightly on.

Guilt clamped down on him as he saw the men in the doorway, and he stared around him in panicked confusion.

148

He was alone in the bed.

Dorian was gone.

"Come on, fella. Let's get moving," one of the men said from the doorway. There were three and they looked like husky marines. They might indeed be the same ones who'd taken him down to the memory-probe that first time. He couldn't tell. They looked as alike as a set of machine-stamped toy soldiers. But he felt relieved. They were just here to escort him down to the lab.

He rose and dressed himself, and then they took him to the same lift as before.

The big room with its floodlights in the center looked unchanged. The big pile of dried-out dirt atumble with flagstones had not been touched. His footprints were still in the dirt. Only the sod had withered and browned.

Men in anonymous jumpsuits stood about in quiet groups. Dorian was not there. He hadn't expected she would be.

A labtech approached, clothing hung over his arm: Frank's original clothes.

As the men watched, Frank, feeling like an animal on display, stripped himself and put on the clothes he'd worn only a week or so earlier.

They felt heavy, cumbersome, awkward, and ill fitting. The material was too tight, too inelastic in his pants. His shirt was tight across his chest. His shoes pinched and rubbed against his heels. His socks bunched at the toes.

His watch felt heavy on his arm. The sweep-second hand was not moving. He absently gave the winding stem a few turns.

Was this stuff really his? The keys and coins in his right pants pocket jangled against his thigh. His wallet was bulky in his left pocket. *All those cards and photos . . .*

They led him into the center of the room, steering him as if he were a sleepwalker. He stepped over cables that twisted here and there like endless snakes. When he climbed up on the pile of earth, he saw the black snout of a new machine pointed at him, looking like the half-remembered projector at the planetarium. And, beyond the glare of lights, a figure in dark robes: Lord Damon. The Heir of Syncom's eyes were masked by goggles, and his face betrayed no expression.

149

The others began pulling down goggles over their eyes, and Frank was told to stand quietly and not move.

He had the crazy notion to raise his finger in an obscene salute at the last moment, but he did not move.

It happened in a single wink.

Chapter Nineteen

THIS IS HOW IT ENDED: no rising whine of generators, no pulsing lights, none of those melodramatic props the low-budget "sci-fi"— horrible word!—movies use. There was no warning at all.

It was as before: In the space of a single instant, the room with its staring goggled labtechs was gone—

—the ground beneath his feet shifted—

—and a summer breeze caressed his cheeks. Above, the bright stars, winking. Close by his ear, the high-pitched hum of a mosquito.

He was standing in his own backyard, back where it all began, back where it had never happened. A huge and throbbing sadness filled him and tears formed in his eyes.

They'd sent him back to a point in time only seconds after the one from which they'd snatched him.

For a brief moment in time, a single flicker in the eyes of anyone who might have been watching, a boy had disappeared and a machine had taken his place—a hulking, grotesque-looking machine of polished blue-black that momentarily reflected the glint of the stars, squatting in a hollowed crater in a suburban American backyard.

He looked around him at all the alien, familiar objects. He shifted his weight, and his shoe dug into the soft broken earth. He filled his chest with air and then released it again. And a tear made a tiny rivulet down one cheek.

The kitchen screen door squeaked open, and his mother's voice called out, "Frank? Are you out here?"

"*Yes, Mother,*" he said, and the vowels of the English language felt thick and clumsy on his tongue. *In all this world, only he could speak that other language.* And already he felt it dying within him.

He'd lost so much!

"—did you hear me? I said Betti's on the phone." His mother's voice sounded like a voice from somewhere in his distant childhood.

"Okay," he said. "Tell her I'll call her back—sometime," his voice trailed off.

Betti's on the phone. Betti, with the bleached hair, too much makeup, a pointy padded bra, and that feverishly coy way of hers, wordlessly telling you that she wanted you to go on, while holding you off, always playing her teasing, deceitful little-girl game.

Betti, who always kept you dangling to let you know she had The Power, that she was the seller in a seller's market, and maybe you'd have to go on the waiting list this week, fella. . . .

Well, the little boy she'd played that sweaty game with didn't live here anymore.

He stamped the dirt from his shoes and swung open the screen door.

He was home.